My

Hero

by Maude Hutchins

GEORGIANA, *A Novel*

A DIARY OF LOVE, *A Novel*

LOVE IS A PIE, *Stories and Plays*

A NEW DIRECTIONS BOOK

MAUDE HUTCHINS

My Hero

For the technical information used about
the Hillman-Minx the author wishes
to express her gratitude to *Motor Cars
Today* by John Harrison, Oxford University
Press.

New Directions books are published
by James Laughlin at Norfolk, Conn.
New York office: 333 Sixth Avenue.

Printed in the United States of America
Designed by Stefan Salter.

First published as New Directions paperback in 2010.
ISBN: 978-0-8112-1899-3

"Others form the man; I tell of him."

MONTAIGNE

"The poets have done well to place a vast interval between
Heaven and Hell. In truth my hand trembles."

DIDEROT *to* GRIMM

"If I had time I could compose a whole litany of anti-
theses."

WERTHER

My

Hero

CHAPTER ONE

I would prefer that he tell his own story, such as it is, not so much a story as a cabala, a secret combination that I have robbed him of, even raped from him and set down now in my own words, not his. I suspect, although I mean him to be the star, that those who read me will also learn about myself, but that is not my intention. My little star, little because in the beginning he was, and star because his mother, pregnant through the winter and spring months finally against her inclination let him go in mid-summer, and poetically interested in astronomy was tempted to, and did name him, Virgo, a summer sign, and a sweet word, i.e., virgin. And so she gave him, too, per-haps, what she herself had lost, and a kind of immortality of purity, too, that she desired. . . . All I can do now, as alter ego, is to attempt to lead the boy backwards, as it were, because he is a man now, to that time when in holy water from the fount he was given a name and in the sign of the cross, too, two thousand years old, in honor of a male virgin who likewise, in time, owing to the precession of the equinoxes has moved backward thirty degrees, so I have been told, and no longer sits in his own constellation but in Libra just west of him.

Three weeks after the birth of the virgin, if a headlong dive, the doctor told me, that sent him spinning through his new element, only to be abruptly checked by the cord and rolled back like a spring, fighting his leash like an undisciplined puppy, nearly strangling himself, can be called a birth—well, no ordinary one anyway—Christina, his mother, completely recovered from her euphoric state, and chastened by the big trauma of childbearing said, "His name is Steve."

"He sure was glad to get OUT," muttered the doctor, "and he sucked in the air like the fish he was, slippery as an eel, his gills workin' like a fluke. Well, I'm off, the blues are bitin', and mark my words," he added, "he don't want to go back." Ahh, "Virgo," I thought, but what did the old fisherman mean? My imagination visualized the quick metamorphosis of fish into man, the sudden symbol, happening in painful and bloody instants, one every minute all over the world: The babe with a full-grown inheritance, including a nine-months refresher course, as it were, imitating in a few moments the evolution of eons, an astonishing metamorphosis of a kind that only the Greeks can tell of calmly. From the purity of darkness to the adultery of light, from the terrific pressure of a tiny oceanus to an atmosphere almost devoid of it. No wonder he falls when he tries to stand, what is there to support him, and yet in a short while his intelligence will intuitively balance him and he may do as he pleases and imagine the rest.

Well, Christina, as I have said, went back to her dishes, not metaphorically but really and truly, and said *sotto voce*, "His name is Steve." I do not know, because I do not know Christina, why, in view of her return to her own peculiar normalcy in the usual period of time, she nevertheless insisted in the chapel that he be baptized after the constellation after all, but she did rather petulantly and stubbornly favor the heathen appellation; and none being present to deny his virginity nor her maternal right to nominate him raised his voice against the anachronism.

There is no good reason other than conventional literary habit to discuss the accidental parents of Virgo; Steve. Nor their four progenitors and the latter's eight, backward into infinite relationship making us all kin, as I believe that he was brand new, an original; good and evil inherent in him and his to decide, given the average opportunity, what would become of him. Certainly nothing as dramatic, unless he imagined it, was likely to occur while he was sober as his own birth, and nothing more mysterious, no matter in what strange recesses he sought, than his own ability asleep or awake, to beget.

But in case something comes of it I will tell the little I know of Christina, his mother, and Samuel, his father, neither of whom he ever got to know very well, which is the reason I know so little worth mentioning. Christina was normal. She washed, ironed, cooked, cleaned, went to bed with Sam. She had one good print dress and four quite handsome sons, counting Steve; the only thing out of the ordinary about her being that her grandfather was the first bishop of the state she was populating, and she kept his mitre and her own counsel, as it were, up attic. Sam, his father, was normal, too; he was a fine mechanic, owned his own garage and did not yearn for that which might be beyond his comprehension. One thing alone set him apart: a violent temper, that seemed to grow and swell in his veins but which no one marked, even himself, until it was too late. Whether this loss of control was inherited, his genes hoarding a chemical passed on to him by a Portuguese sailor, I would not want to state categorically, but that his papa was a guitar-playing passionate nomad who chanced to penetrate the rocky coast of Maine, temporarily casting his nets for livelihood and of necessity taking to bed for the moment a down-east school teacher whom he left at dawn to catch the tide, I have learned not from Virgo but from Sam's neighbors of a generation ago, who felt that Sam did have a drop or two of "foreign" blood in him but forgave him his impulses because he was successful and trustworthy and went to church on Sunday. No pilgrim, it is true, but "live and let live."

Nothing, I suppose, will happen that has not happened before. Steve will subsist for a little while longer on the monotonous diet that Christina will provide. Dependent on her for a little while longer he will eat of Christina and she will tolerate this cannibalism because of the pleasure it gives her. She will never love him again as she did while he was inside her; she had no desire to dominate this new man any more than she did the others. She fed them and fed them well and let them go their ways. She kept her own counsel, as I have said, and a mitre up attic. Two years after Virgo she christened a little daughter, her last child, "Anna" for no poetic reason and returned to her men. And so the choreography of Steve's life will begin as usual; that fourth wall, as the curtain in the theatre is called, has folded up and slid away and he is visible. I shall try from the sporadic instances he has told me of, and my own insight, to let you have Steve, for the nonce. My only outline which is before me, reads: "From: (1) innocence; to: (2) carnal knowledge; to: (3) ideal love; to: (4) reality; to: (5) his code of behavior, 'I harm no one, so it is not bad.' " This candid quotation and simple logic is Steve's. Everything but the code, so *reductio ad absurdum* as to be idiotic, in the sense of genius, is an outline or super-structure, a scaffolding on which one might write or think of anyone, male or female, who in turn might hang him or herself upon it or build themselves a castle, God willing. There is no hint of the secret mixture in this plan; of the cabala, that will make of Steve an in-dividual, a mysterious unit, a hand dealt from a deck of cards that may never reappear.

There is one thing, however, I feel in honor bound as an artist to admit, perhaps confess: If my story of Steve is not true, if you do not understand it, if you remain cold and do not love him . . . well, I loved him at the time I set it down, not as one must love one's hero in any fiction, but as I loved him in my own life, the choreography of which will not appear except unintentionally, and which may well have been only a story within a story, something he invented because he, too, loved me, and made me for the time being a heroine, speaking with my own mouth his thoughts, and as now his mouth will tell, who knows, my story.

To begin with, the littlest girl in his life, the first recognizable form that stepped out of the chaos, as it were, of his own secret mixture that made him want more than glory—love, which so far (in his own words, "Well, I found out that it worked") lacked an objective—was a passionate little brat who when he kissed her, each of them six, said, "It feels like riding my bike." "What did it feel like to you?" I asked Steve and I felt a pin prick of jealousy when he said without hesitation, "It was the most wonderful feeling in the world; I have never felt it just like that since; it was overwhelming." I have set myself a difficult task, I see, writing Steve's or any man's story; how much easier to write about that little woman. "It feels like riding my bike." Now that is specific and original and sensual; the reader straddles his bike at the age of six and re-

members, identifies himself or herself with the little sen-
sualist and from then on it is simple to hold his or her
attention. But Steve's, "It was wonderful; it was overwhelming," is too meteorological, too general, too superla-
tive, and so I can only give you Steve through the women
in his life about whom he will tell me himself.

It was only yesterday that I asked Steve, "Tell me some
more about Ginger's 'kiss,' " and he said, "All I can remember is it felt good," and I did not insist, "Be specific,"
because I could not and did not want to turn him into a
woman, spoiling my story; it is hard enough keeping my
female identification out of it as it is. Ginger's love feelings, so readily and naïvely expressed (I am sure as she
grew up she learned to hold her tongue), so geographical,
as it were, and Steve's male, and I am afraid, deeper, purer,
indigenous reaction while the first kiss lasted are that
difference, perhaps, that builds up into the tantalizing
inequality between the sexes. Ginger, the woman, put her
finger, as it were, on it; Steve, the male, more anatomically
specific, one would think, put his heart into it, and the one
felt a tiny thrill, nuclear, the other was "overwhelmed"
and didn't know one part of him from another. It wasn't
that she was cleverer and could express herself better, was
it? I don't think so. Steve was "under a spell"; Ginger
was sober and made a note of her feelings instanter.

This Ginger, it appears, was not a little girl easy to
forget, if he wanted to forget her, I don't know, but she
was, I gather, that poltergeist, placed, it seems, by nature,

in one's early life, very early in Steve's, ubiquitous, just to get one used in the beginning to the big irritations and future frustration that come with maturity, so you don't blow your top then. Her vulgar giggles with her girl friends in his presence, her lying, her pig-latin and secret sorority, her patronizing airs and efficiency in little things, her teaching him to cheat, her total collapse when caught in any act, her carefully planned, it seemed, alienation of his friends, exasperated the little fellow; but her rapid changes of demeanor, her solemn little oval face in church, her penetrating sweet voice, her ginger-colored hair— well, her terrible magnetism, I imagine—as he later put it, "cast a spell" over him. But I remember he said at another time, "She was like a piece of sandpaper." His irritation must have been almost too much to bear, but whether he was able to or not did not remain to be seen because she moved away. Then she began to become in earnest, to Steve, that "first love" that lasts forever as they always do, the image getting smaller and smaller but clearer and clearer like looking through the wrong end of a telescope so that he felt like a liar at forty when he protested, "I love you best," to whomever it was he really loved at the time.

But even Ginger, it seems to me, comes relatively late in Steve's love-life. Don't we all know, either from being told so, or reading it, or actually remembering it, that love begins with life itself, divisible, it is true, into just plain reflex, passion, sentiment, devotion, habit; sacred and pro-

fane, as it were, good and evil all mixed up. The only thing
missing at the age, say, of two weeks: the sweet ability to
daydream, that atmospheric, almost, epitome of love;
neither, I suppose, does the little creature, no bigger than
the dimensions of his mother's hips, and no wiser than the
family dog, enjoy any anticipation or look back with
pleasure on anything. I think only a vague uneasiness
informs his frontal lobes that it's time to eat and the table
is at hand. And so, as I have said, from fish to mammal,
he begins now to enjoy along with his mother's milk an
entertainment, his first floor show. Will he ever kiss as
well as this again, giving and receiving pleasure? How
indolent he looks, how pink he has become, and the
pleasure isn't localized in his mouth; if only Ginger were
here and could describe her feelings, but to Steve, I suppose, it was "overwhelming." No wonder a man can never
find a pie like the pie that mother used to make, and this
harmless desire descended from such a powerful memory
we should all try to satisfy, lest our man try another
tavern. And can a woman understand the struggle a lad
goes through to leave this lovely console, conscious or unconscious; won't he prefer a member of his own sex, next?
Wouldn't that be easier, better, less wanton? I doubt if
I'll get anything out of Steve on this important point so
what about me, how would I feel? But this something
no amount of self-identification with my "character" will
approximate in my imagination. I can have no insight.
Still I can't help thinking that girls should nurse their

fathers; then they would understand better, be nicer, kinder, less critical, not shocked at something that never entered their heads or senses. *"Hircus Civis Eblamensis! He had buckgoat paps on him, soft ones for orphans."* (Joyce.) Girls have a better chance, if we're talking about propriety, because they don't feel guilty about wanting to suckle their mothers at all, they just get bored after awhile and turn to the opposite sex like turning from one side of the bed to the other, and it's natural, not unnatural. There won't be any punishment. But if the little female nursed the male, then she would desperately seek one of her own shape a little later, wouldn't she? As it is, she often does, anyway, as a variable in that in-between bisexual age, indeterminate and sulky, underprivileged and discontent. Why does she "anyway"? because it is easier? more of the same? Or is it, having suckled and fondled her mother without success, as it were, does she yearn to master the image of her passive parent just once, before the inevitable return to reality: just lying down and taking it; domination, not only in what she must become but domination from on high, almost, "woman stand and be counted"; your passions are dictated by your shape and your anatomy makes you what you are. You may, and will, pursue the male only when his back is turned.

Well, isn't it a good thing Steve was weaned before his sharp teeth penetrated the gums, or wouldn't he have, unable to distinguish between the relativity of his desires, ate her up? Some boy children, I understand, dream and fear that their fathers are going to eat them. Is this a savage juxtaposition of images? Gargantua, Rabelais, a big infant, himself, tells us, was born out of his mother's ear, like a weasel, but I never saw a picture or heard tell of him trying to get back that way although I've seen plenty of the more normal attempts of other fictional heroes.

I maintain that this first period of Steve's life, let us call it his nutritional period, was innocent; I do not believe that the old Adam is his tutor until baptism or that he would trot back to Hell as fast as his little legs would take him if he should die before he was wetted on the forehead and blessed in the name of the Father, the Son, and the Holy Ghost. Love yes, evil no. I have not said "platonic" as to Steve, however; the only platonic love is a fish's prerogative, if a fish has a choice, and his only pleasure the thrill of swimming up stream to fertilize the egg alone, the earliest and saltiest masturbation on record.

I will take Steve away now from his mother's breast, especially as you have heard that at the age of six, without being asked, he attacked the mouth of Ginger, and mutually hungry they enjoyed the abstraction of kissing, abstracted as it was from an earlier and more practical performance but conditioned by that survival instinct to something else which had become more urgent. And from now on each might starve if, miraculously enough, the pangs of hunger did not follow like an echo, a memory, instead of precede, the little act of love. We aren't, although they come to mind, going to talk about those monsters who, never conditioned, overeat, mistakenly thinking that food alone will bring them satisfaction; security I believe it is called.

I wonder why, returning to me, partly because I can't help it and partly because my intelligence tells me that without understanding myself I can't understand Steve or anyone for that matter, I didn't, as Steve did, find a little contemporary lover at that age, his age; when having left the maternal bosom, first the womb and then the bosom, a child, conditioned as it has been, seeks the condition itself. And having forgotten that there was such a little person in my life, and Steve not as yet having told me about La Ginger, knowing there must have been someone and thinking that it must have been someone much older because with me it was (so I thought), I asked him, "Can't you remember; wasn't there a woman early in your life who seduced your imagination; how did you avoid such a chance encounter?"

"No," said Steve.

"But with me," I said, "I was in love with a middle-aged man when I was eight; a commuter!" and I laughed. Yes, I remember I used to listen for his train, and imagine that I, his little wife, young it is true, but faithful, talented, brave, would meet him at the end of the road, meet the bus that dropped him off at the corner, and I did; I never missed it, and the nonchalance I pretended was my

first self-discipline, deceit for the benefit of my mother
who wondered why I felt the need to take a walk before
supper. I can still see him swinging off the hind step of
that bus, his briefcase hanging from his hand, and hear
the shift of gears as the bus went on and his, "Hello, Suzie."
I learned to take long steps like his. He gave me very
little, I realize now, other than that two-minute companion-
ship by his side, in silence, and sometimes the time was
shortened by his real wife's coming a little ways to meet
him. I thought she was a very inferior person and did not
deserve him. I would have taken him away from her
without the least remorse; I was fresh out of the egg and
predatory. As it was, somebody else did; "a fly-by-night"
I heard her called by that wife of his who whined out her
abandonment to the neighbors, set a detective on his trail
and pathetically, I think now, attempted to solve the problem of his walk-out by dwelling on her daily life last
week, the week before, and the week before that. "How
was I to know that . . . ?" and "How could I possibly
realize considering . . . ?" and "Why didn't he tell me that
he preferred black coffee?" "I didn't *know* he liked
oysters." "I remember *now* that queer look he gave me
when I forgot to take the *curlers* out of my hair." "I don't
suppose I should have *bothered* him with the servant
problem; I didn't have anybody to *tell* anything to all
day, though; maybe it wasn't very *interesting*." "I used
to ask him what happened at the office; I would have
liked to hear his troubles but he just said 'nothing,'

or 'you wouldn't be interested.' " "I didn't want another child but he didn't seem to care about *that;* maybe if I had had another; the others, though, seemed to annoy him more than anything else." "I thought he wanted to be with *me,* now that they were off at school. And he worried so, at least I thought he didn't *like* me to be sick." "I had diarrhea all night once but I got up and had breakfast with him; I was weak as a stick but I laughed, I was quite funny." "What do you suppose?" "When, at what *point* in our relations did he . . . ?" "At what *time* did he *change?*" and she actually looked at her watch as if she only knew, that the rest would become clear. "If I only knew the exact *time.*"

"Why don't you call off the police, dear," said my mother kindly.

"It isn't the police, it's a detective."

"Why don't you call him off, dear," my mother repeated. "It isn't very sporting is it, I'm sorry."

"But how can I find him by myself?"

"What would you do if you did?"

"I'd *ask* him *why?*"

"And then what?"

" 'Why?' That's all."

"Would you take him back?"

"Oh, never!"

I remember all of this strange conversation and many others perfectly. I began to identify myself with the deserted wife; I no longer considered her volubility, weakness; nor her wanting to get at him just to *ask* him, ridiculous. But she did call off the detective as soon as the first shock, making her almost crazy, receded. And then one day I told a story:

("Why? Why?" she was saying passionately three weeks later, as she held her cup of tea, unsweetened, untouched, and peered into my mother's face for an answer. I sat with my own little cup of tea under the tea table, my legs stretched out, as I always did.)

"I saw him," I said.

My mother looked down under the leaf of the table at me. I could feel her eyes on the back of my neck. I was facing the deserted wife and she carefully but shakily put her cup down. Her eyes looked—well, at first—startled, then a flush came up from her throat and suffused her face, turning it bright pink. I was frightened, because she looked as if she had got a letter at the post office. Yes, I saw hope in her face.

"He was with a woman," I said. "He looked very sad and as if he was not going to speak to me, but I said, 'Hello,' and he said, 'Hello, Suzie,' very low. He was very pale. He got right off the trolley car after that, with her. He tipped his hat to me first." My mother touched me with her slipper, "Go to your room, Suzan," and as I started away, "What trolley car?"

"In New York," I answered, "Forty-second Street."

"You have never been in New York. Will you say good-by to Mrs. Cassells now?"

"What a little liar you were," said Steve and he seemed pleased, looking inward, it seemed to me, but just as he was about to speak I foolishly interrupted his thoughts, but not before denying it, "No," I said, "it was true, I did see him, he was pale, there was a woman, he did tip his hat, he did say, 'Hello, Suzie.'"

"But the trolley car; Forty-second Street?"

"I don't know but I swear it was true, how could I remember it so long?"

"The trolley car," said Steve.

"That was how I had to prove it," I said with sudden insight that was no good to anyone but me. "That was the only part a grown-up would understand, 'a trolley car, Forty-second Street'; it was true that the trolley car was false, Forty-second Street made up, but he *was* pale."

"Tell me really and truly, Steve," I said, "wasn't there an equivalent in your childhood to my commuter? a school teacher, a neighbor's wife, the maid?"

He picked out the key word, maid, in his mind, and laughed, "The maid! My mother was the maid!"

"That's what I mean."

"What?"

"Your mother then, an unrequited and passionate, impossible and improbable attachment to your mother? Christina?"

"Hell, no."

I have lost the thread of my logic, but didn't he subconsciously mean that his mother was a virgin; to him?

Don't we, lots of times, say simple ordinary things, but doesn't the language, itself, make our meaning clearer than we mean it to be? Aren't all our *faux pas* big with meaning? Doesn't the very word *pas* mean *step; a step* preceded weakly by *false?* censoring ourselves quick like that. Steve had picked up a copy of *Vogue* and was staring at an ad. "Falsies," he said.

"Steve, tell me about your mother; your mother and you; what did she look like, for instance?"

"I honestly don't know."

We didn't seem to be getting anywhere at all and my intuition told me (in fact it said quite clearly, "Don't be stupid!") that direct questioning brings out the "no" in any human animal, but I persisted, against these intellectual cautions, "What was the first thing that frightened you; way back, way, way, back? Do you remember? I remember me, for instance, I was afraid of the smell of ammonia from an uncorked bottle, and a can-opener, and once when. . . ."

"It was confusion. . . ." interrupted Steve.

"Well!" I thought, "A big word again."

"Noise! Horrible!"

I didn't say anything but waited.

"My mother . . . ."

"His mother" (to myself).

"My mother tied me to a pole, you can't blame her, I suppose she thought . . . ."

"No, it was stupid."

"She had to cure me, I guess she thought, I was so afraid of trains. 'Come here,' she said; her hands were behind her back; I was already scared because the 2:08 was due; I say that now because I know, but then I didn't *know* why I was scared *beforehand* like that . . . suppose the 2:08 hadn't come through that day," he asked himself.

"My dog . . . ." I interrupted; (I am not a very good listener).

"She was strong and quick; she stooped down and grabbed me all over."

"Yes," I thought, "he could see her big divided breasts; it was summer and her dress was cut low; he felt her soft breasts and her hard thighs and longed to throw his arms around her neck and love her; but she would think he was begging for mercy which he would not do, he wasn't like that, he would certainly take it, whatever was coming, at that 'come here,' with no smile, no quarter, or doubt in her demeanor. Whatever it was, she had thought it through."

"She tied me to the pole beside the track."

With his sister Anna's jumping rope (I thought), she tied a good strong square knot or a granny, maybe, and tucked the red wooden handles, still sticky with cinnamon candy, back under and around the rope, with some difficulty too, she had him tied so tight. "Breathe in," she said coolly, and drew it even closer. For the short time it took her to finish, he lost his awful fear of the train and felt anger; he hated her. She stood up, taking the perfume

of her hair and body away with her—the sun was shining
smack down on her head and gave her a luminous tri-
colored halo—and looked at the watch she wore swinging
from a pin on the left side of her chest. That watch, that
mechanical heart, that he had so often heard, louder and
more acute (tick! tock!) than the sound of Christina's
own heart. When he was littler she had held him close
and he had felt the swelling, deeper, thrilling rhythm of
the real thing, but since he could walk, the mechanical
ticking of his mother's watch was as close as he could get
to her. He used to practice, all his senses in his ears, and
gradually, eliminating everything else, the mechanical
heart would greet him as he came in the door of the house.
Over and above everything: the bigger clock on the wall,
the throbbing of other mechanisms in the house, the toilet,
the drip of the kitchen faucet, his sister's foolish double
talk.

His mother turned and went away. She did not look
back. She was strong; strength itself. She had timed things
well: As her back was eclipsed by the front door, a great
uproar that shook the ground beneath him, that shattered
the air about him, that tensed his muscles as if a great set
of weights squeezed him together from all directions, burst
out of the west, straight at him. He saw it like a huge eye
with no whites, it filled the dimensions of his universe; it
was All. Cosmos; Chaos. He became violently excited; it
crippled the imagination and it seemed, speedily as it
thundered on, to hesitate with each tremendous beat of his

caged and aching heart. Like some evil poetry, it advanced toward him in gulping iambic. Ahhhhh. . . . It spat by him like a huge hiccough in his bowels, but not such a clamor that he didn't distinctly hear in his ears, on the inner side of his ears, his brave words; his spiritual denial of the power of evil before he fainted at 2:08, "Lick my shit."

I am reminded of the lost emotional formula of that race of horses that instinctively, when exhausted beyond endurance, open a vein with their teeth, in order to breathe. But Steve was saved by some sort of built-in safety device; a little army of genes, perhaps, was marching in his blood to his defense. He didn't even take to his bed for supper; he ate as usual with good appetite, played outside till dark; but that night he had a divine dream, the subject of which he was never able to place, ever, but the whole dreamy episode, he slowly woke and knew, was sweet to excess, and a delicious almost penitential sadness soothed the little novice back to sleep. A pitch black slumber this time that blotted out the consciousness of this tiny genesis of things to come, this lonely self-seduction, this consuming consummation between, I suppose, two impersonations, one might say, the I and the me of him; a bivalve-boy of that symbolic period I told you about that he spent in the Deep.

Well, and so the cord was broken a second time and he won't go back, as I am reminded the old doctor said to me, "He don't *want* to." And the next time the nocturnal vision was not conditioned. He didn't remember having been

frightened by anything the day before. He outdistanced
the train, as it were, walked away from the tragedy.

And, Ginger, the little red-headed female, the sandpaper
girl, I have had moved away from him, you remember. It
is true he will keep her in an old watch, as it were, but
her sticky little personality and bad manners she really
took with her.

Ginger . . . . I had denied that in my own childhood
there had been a little contemporary of the opposite sex
but as I persuaded Steve to tell me of an equivalent passion, as unknowingly he had, to my weaker, positively
adulterated, one for a balding commuter, swinging off a
noisy bus (not having nursingly desired my father), it
came to me, out of chronological order, mixing up my
literary sequence, that there had been a vivid little Jew,
a bicycle riding (too!), satin-skinned biped, male, who
had kissed me on the mouth; longingly, not masterfully;
but ingratiating; sickening me. I was not "overwhelmed"
except mildly repelled. I shivered in his thin arms that
triangled me; I imagined his rib-basket under his coat, like
a chicken's, and chicken-hearted, too. Our bodies did not
touch. The only attraction I had felt for him was ruined
for good by that wet and trembling kiss; and the pleading
looks he bent on me in the following weeks angered me;
I did not feel womanly pity, even, or maternal solicitude,
for my skinny conquest; but he, too, it came back to me,
taught *me*; to cheat! Just as Ginger, Steve had told me,
without any details of course, had tutored him; but I think

that Ginger infiltrated Steve, and metaphorically, as it were; while Sydney, son of an accountant, gave me the answers to mathematical problems, passing them back to me under the myopic gaze of the teacher who waited patiently for the end of the term to chastise us with her *post-facto* knowledge gained on the spot, "Did you children think I was *blind?*" "No. Only cock-eyed," I said to myself. I accepted his gift of numbers and I felt a sickly pleasure in doing so. I don't know why; the anemic pleasure of sublimation perhaps. I gave him nothing in return although I excelled in other subjects that he found difficult, and he never seemed to expect an exchange of gifts. The cheating together, I think, gave him physical pleasure; my secret passivity warmed his blood, made him forget my cold, almost insolent, indifference to him in the other little social circumstances of our school days. No, Sydney is not in any old watch of mine and if he were, the snapshot, I am afraid, would remind me now as it did then, unfortunately, of my dog; that three-legged stance of any dog, any time; that's what Sydney looked like hiking his hind leg up over his bicycle before he was off, "So long!"; lonely, and as I realize now, rather sweet, a nice lad, slight and brooding. Am I in his watch?

CHAPTER TWO

Important as it is to get on with the pattern, Steve's and mine, which has become dual now, which is, I suppose, inevitable, although I did not plan it . . . while my little oriental is moving along on his bike past me, one foot down, now, on the gravel, slowing up his going away, staring into my eyes; a curving smile, slim bony fingers gripping the handle bars, dawdling . . . dawdling . . . not saying anything (didn't Ginger move off more decisively?), I long, contrarily, to recall the little spectre; be kind to him, half-way decent, make him happy. (Sidney, Sidney, come back, I have a T.L. for you.) Didn't a young aunt in a hurry, with Egypt in her dreamy eyes, and more bosom than I, seduce him after a while in the hen house anyway? keeping the blood intact, in the family, as it were? and flowing in an unadulterated stream out of Israel and back again; saving up the features, preserving the manners, upholding the *mores*, donating a pint to the great, brave, and resistant Race; opinionated, caressing a big doctrine; Orthodox? Well, So long, indigo-hair and chocolate-eyes, others have formed you and I cannot tell of you. I am involved with a little occidental, born under the sixth sign of the zodiac, which is situated on the celestial equator due south of the handle of the dipper. But none of us sees the same thing in the sky, and even the conclusions of astrological adepts are far from uniform, so I am told. But Virgo is still virgin; his first girl off on her own business in her own orbit and he has twice set himself free from Christina, if he ever imagined a servitude, I don't know; but I think he did. And Christina has certainly, not unthinkingly, but unknowingly, allied herself with tragedy in Steve's subconscious. My grown-up Steve is not, it appears, very introspective, "I was too busy being a boy to remember it," neither does he dwell on the past and this period of his life of which I am telling—this pre-adolescent era, after Ginger and before the visionary one, that ideal love that comes next on the agenda, was one of transition; from innocence, which I called his nutritional period, to carnal knowledge; he ate the apple. An insinuating harvest only, in his fondling of Ginger, that left him unappeased but took his appetite away, nevertheless; then thrust upon him by his first nocturnal experience prefaced by a "divine" dream and followed by more zealous daylight investigations ("Well, I found out it worked"). None of these experiments seems to have left any indelible mark for good or evil on his character or in his memory. True, it was playtime, uninhibited, at least it appeared to

be, and whether it was reaction from something, or preparation for something, I can't exactly say, but the succeeding
days until long after dark were filled with a succession of
naughtiness; the typical, I think, monkeyshines of little
men. "What are little boys made of," sing-songed Anna.
"Rats and snails and puppy dog tails!" The four boys eyed
Anna. One's heart stands still! Why didn't they tear her to
bits? they could have!

"Tattletale!"

"Let's go."

And all the little boys in town who in a few years would
be "overwhelmed" by duplicate Annas, no doubt, the
Bubbles and Dodos, had slammed as many doors and were
off; something impelling them to practice savagery in va-
cant lots, barns, and on the highways; in the garden and
on the roof, and to swipe the candles from the altar as an
extra sensation, and to light up a supper of stolen dog
biscuits rifled from a box car, before entering into mys-
teries that were more specific: Group seizures that paled
the mythological phantasies of the gods. If they had
painted their faces red and gilt their bodies, they might
have passed for a hatch of Dionysi, or a choir of Pygmies
practicing imitative magic in honor of Atys. Incontinence
otherwise uncountenanced, and excesses for a reason: to
make the grain grow and propitiate the vine: honoring
fecundity, a word these lads couldn't even spell; which
is the only way I can think of to describe the orgies of the
ornery little brothers and sons of us women, who can only

sit by and gasp and watch the clock for a merciful passage of time; and sublimation into commuters, maybe, a back and forth bloodless imitation, too, of the seasons, death and resurrection: from the security of home and mother to the freedom of Wall Street and Tammany Hall, Macy's and Gimbel's; what do you think?

"It's a phase" "It will pass" "Little hoodlums" "Naughty boys." But who could guess to what depths, hand in hand, it had descended, this little gilded oligarchy, or to what heights it had risen? Just exactly like the gods they unconsciously and sympathetically mimicked and as the gods themselves imitated the seed, itself. On the other hand, scrubbed and neatly dressed on Sundays and holidays, aren't they like the geode on my desk? that secretive stone that looks like any other rock but when you open it, is lined with miniature stalactites and stalagmites of lustrous pink crystals; in its turn analogous, in opposition to the mythological and sylvan satyr whose outside belies his inside: Beauty and goodness is found inside these goat-legged, self-indulgent and sensual beasties, if you split them in two. It's well worth your while, according to Plato.

Only statistically do I implicate Steve in these Saturnalia; he must have certainly been present; he was normal. I positively cannot remember and have never heard of any similar "games" or Bacchantes among my girl friends, comparable to these festivals and these naughty viviparates finding out about polygamy, maybe.

Certainly monogamous, the little girls I knew seemed to skip the savage concord of their brothers and waged whatever war there was between the sexes in secret sorority that is still a secret, perhaps *the* secret, the mystery; (the search for the possession of which, in perpetuity, keeps the male on his toes, as harmless a metaphor for philandering as I can think of at present); which is, isn't it, the only advantage (strategy) allotted the female? I don't mean that women, to men . . . , men who are poets, anyway, don't believe that woman is the mystery; and not all men ignorantly attempt to possess the unpossessable, as mystery by definition must remain chaste and impervious. Just plain men attack the body which to poets is the symbol and wonder why, next morning, the mystery is still there. This is that old procuress's, mother nature's, finger in the pie and she's not disinterested either. But all men; anyway the male generically, I think, feels that woman will intercede for him; that she is closer to "grace" than he is . . . . Even Ginger?

Well, whatever the little sisters were whispering about, isn't it a good thing that the battle, artifice in one camp and action in the other, never came to bloodshed! The twain didn't tangle. And much later the girl graduates will be called alumnae and the boys, alumni, prosaic and decent appellations; the one still whispering, the other, vicariously, at least, playing football. I said monogamous meaning *à deux*. Little girls don't ever confide in, or play with, the group. They cleave to one at a time. Jean led me

onto a grassy place under an apple tree; I could look up
and see the underside of the blossoms, pale pink, that
dropped straight down on us as we played. She initiated
me. What a strange, entrancing game it was! But she said,
"Don't tell," and I never have. I am an alumna of the occult. With beating heart I accepted my diploma and my
little responsibilities, vested in me.

"You expect me to talk but you won't," Steve said to
me, as I was recollecting these phenomena to myself.

"But there's nothing to tell," I said, "really nothing,
girls aren't like boys."

"They have the same feelings."

"Have they really?"

"Haven't they?"

"I don't know."

"They do the same things, don't they?"

"No, they don't *do*, we are the passive sex, you know,
we don't *do*."

And Steve gave up. "Look here at this adiabatic chart,"
he said, "it shows pressure plotted against temperature."
(He didn't find *that* in *Vogue*.) "That's how it works," he
added.

"Oh, I know how it works," I said, amused at my hidden
reference.

"You *do?*"

"No, I told you I didn't," I grinned. I loved my double talk, but Steve was staring at an engraving of the first pump.

However, a little later, he said, "You know that flowers have orgasm." He spoke softly, out of context; and, startled, I blushed; but I have that secretive skin, olive; it doesn't tell tales; only my eyes felt like warm coals. Steve is a skilled amateur horticulturist and among other things he cultivates his garden. "It's natural," he said, . . . "lilies . . ."

"Yes, it certainly pertains to nature," I thought to myself, but I had just been visualizing nature as an old procuress, with a motive. Now what need in the world . . . what's to be gained by? . . . has a lily? Is it the air that troubles them? Has the atmosphere sweeter and more penetrating densities at one time than another? Before a storm, perhaps, or after it has cleared? South wind? Millibars! What about dew-point? convection? occlusion? I never caught a lily in the act; I'm going to watch! I thought it was bees! Isn't it wonderful . . . .

"Isn't it wonderful?" I said out loud.

"Yes, it is," said Steve seriously.

"And I thought mother nature was just a pompous efficiency expert without any imagination."

"Not so efficient."

"And wasteful."

"That's right."

"Largesse but no *taste*."

"I don't know about that, but she doesn't seem to have any more control over the weather than I have."

"I'm glad she lacks taste or there wouldn't be any artists, just photographers."

"That hard frost hit my Mayduke cherry just as the fruit was forming, right after that gale took off the blossoms."

"Stupid."

"Ruthless, anyway."

"And no proper distortion, just tricks, like foreshortening and perspective and mirages. And that sunset last night! Vulgar."

"Corn has cancer."

"But, Steve?"

"Yes?"

"Flowers? Really? Have you noticed how roses, and lilies too, lilies especially, don't just smell sweet when you want them to, not all the time. Just sometimes, when you're reading a book and not paying any attention, it suddenly comes to you, the perfume, so heady and sweet. Then you look up from your book and they are trembling. But when you go over and sniff them, all you get is a little pollen dust on your nose like gold leaf. Do you suppose the perfume; that that's when . . . ?"

"Maybe."

"But in church!" I whispered, and added, "What shocking bad taste! Do you suppose the Reverend Calhoun knows?"

"I doubt it."

"Steve, do you love me?"

"You know I do."

CHAPTER THREE

Collage Sérieux is the heading of this chapter in Steve's life, not the visionary one I said was next on the agenda but a serious affair nevertheless. You can't expect Steve to tell a chronological story of his life and besides it isn't time for Her. He is only fifteen, just past the cops and robbers regime, the violence and savagery, the solemnly pledged little obscenities, the kicking around of taboos before he decides for himself what he will and will not do. And you remember what he chose, whether neatly put in words or just felt, "I harm no one, so it is not bad." At what point, for him to make this moral statement, good and bad, as such, became divisible, as it were, to him, I don't know. But at fifteen, I am not sure, but I think, he made a moral choice between the sexes and so he selected a boy as his spiritual and physical companion and embraced him. Either he hadn't got over Ginger, repelled by her spiritual infirmity; maybe Christina's cruelty still left its mark on him; maybe he felt that woman and tragedy were inseparable; perhaps just a third try to beat the inevitable return to the Deep, or just a little man's desire for peace and quiet. We mustn't forget, "I harm no one, so it is not bad." I suppose this motto, this almost pledge, was not engraved upon his shield until much later, because it does imply a suspicion of his ability to harm, at least, a potential or probable evil that he must avoid. That must have come with maturity. He was a good boy. He ate the apple, but he did not don a fig leaf; neither then, metaphorically, or to this day does he seem to feel any shame whatever, or make any furtive attempt to hide any part or parts of his body. He is as nude, weather permitting, as Adam before the fall; as a mast on a ship. Carnal knowledge came to him at first in a seductive and divine dream, and he soon acquired a skill, but attended in his dream as he was by some angelic supervision, seduced by a heavenly governess of some sort, I don't know, he remained pure and good. Perhaps Christina, busy with menus, drowsy with attendance on her men, letting down the frocks of Anna, never caught him in the act. Deliberately didn't, maybe; Christina must have known most of what there is to know about the male and his habits and what could she do, cut off the head of a hydra-headed monster, as it were, that would grow back faster than her imagination could chop? Christina accepted the limitations of her feminine culture; that is what made her a good wife; and a feminine sophistication, not learned in night clubs, cautioned her against shaming her man, ever.

"Don't," a voice said when she herself said, "I know what he's up to . . . . But I mustn't catch him, or I could never look him in the eye again, because his eyes would be lowered, and God protect me from being my man's superior and mentor; I prefer to be loved, if that's what it is." Tangent minded, maybe, but at least she didn't present Steve with a liability to penalty; he was guiltless. This intuitive wisdom she practiced in sexual matters only, of course, intuitive because women's intuition is certainly feminine; it stems from sex, like protective coloring, like a cat's whiskers, a moth's antennae; it's a kind of ectoplasm that precedes her and lets her know before she gets there. Christina was simple and forthright and didn't acknowledge hypens or half-notes in other things. Tying a lad to a pole to cure him of effeminacy, almost (that's what she thought fear was), was another matter. Anna's terror of banshees in the bathroom and hop-toads underfoot was not disciplined. But "Don't straddle, it isn't ladylike," Anna often heard. Christina believed that the sexes were separate and definitive. Well, whether or not she knew what Steve was up to, I know she let him finish, and I very much think that the heavenly shine in his eyes and the soft, almost feline, flexibility of his movements after the fact made her heart beat a little faster, as mine does when Steve, my Steve now, . . . but I must tell you before I go on with the little Steve's adolescence just one story that he told me today when I was no longer trying to probe him on his former bantam existence, his little cockhood, his naughty

excursions. My eavesdropping, as all literary effort has to
be, I suppose, on Christina and Sam, had not exposed
either of them to the little three dimensional pictorial history he told me about because it amused him. It is called
The Magnolia Tree.

"Dad used to take me to see a lady; I used to enjoy it;
I don't remember where it was, but I suppose Dad had a
girl friend. She was a widow; I can still remember what
she looked like. He used to leave me outside while he went
in; he said he'd be right out; he never stayed very long.
There was a big magnolia tree in the yard and I climbed
up into it and looked in the window, not because I was
expecting to see anything, or find out anything, but just
to look. Dad came to the window and I never saw him so
mad! His face was purple! I was scared. 'You get down
out of that magnolia tree before I skin your hide!' I
dropped out of it, believe me, 'bang!' "

I saw him in my imagination obeying Newton's law. I
laughed. I saw also his father's apopletic face and behind
the lace curtains, back on the untidy bed, the widow; the
widow Steve remembered just what she looked like; but
not from his perch that day, other times; but he couldn't
remember any other times except the times he waited outside "not very long," so I don't think he ever saw her
really. But in his imagination he may have had as clear an
image of his father's mistress as I have now: lying on her
side, one hip uncovered, on an untidy bed, with a thin
pillow, the ticking showing. The bed lies parallel with

the wall opposite the window, furthest away from the light, and although the sun is shining on the magnolia tree and the little boy like an inquisitive monkey in its branches surrounded by pink blossoms, it is gray in the room; a single bulb in the ceiling doesn't distribute any light even though it is on. The widow is also almost blacked out by the big frame of Sam in the window bawling at Steve, "Get the hell out of that magnolia tree!" and grayish lace curtains, a little stiff from starch, fall back from Sam's shoulders like the sea in the wake of a ship. So you see I didn't get a very clear picture of the widow. But she was round in places, the uncovered hip was smooth and pink, more so than her face which was pale as if she was never out of the room; and bluish shadows, the color of skimmed milk, were under and over her eyes, in the small hollows of her face and neck. Her hair is the same tone as she is, with no depths in it, due, I suppose, to the strange indirect lighting in the room. Perhaps she would be, outdoors, or under a top light, an entirely different shape and color, someone else. Inside, she did seem to lack a dimension, I don't know which.

"Was her hair black, blonde, brown?" I asked Steve.

"I couldn't tell you."

"Was she nice to you?"

"I never saw her."

"But?"

"I mean . . . ."

So you see Steve's picture of her was one that slept inside him, clear enough but lost, like a familiar word that can't be spoken. That is it, I think, or else the little boy in the magnolia tree imagined a symbol, rather than a realistic colored postcard of the lady; something took shape in his mind; phallic? I don't know; it is lost now, anyway.

Steve didn't tell me easily about the lad and himself, but not because he felt culpable. I don't think the male lives in the past as much, at least doesn't nostalgically return to his youth and its sensations, as a woman with time on her hands, daydreaming backwards when she is grown up as she used to frontwards when she was a girl, does. A man's busyness fills his mind while a woman, even a busy one, is reminded by everything she handles of something else, and that else is part of a daydream. Every window I look out of reminds me of another window I looked out of, every horse another horse I mounted, every door knob some other door knob, a kind of continuous and collective experience, even a fickle, perhaps, disassociation of things, smells, colors and shapes; and that is why I never really belonged to one man, how could I honestly say so, when the smell of him behind his ear reminded me of another, . . . and that one's coat as I lay against it set a tune off in my head. "My love works in a GREENhouse and on his coat laPEL is the Odor of VIOlets, gerAniums as WELL . . . ," and that tune X used to sing. No, I am not all there, if you want to take advantage of that. But this is Steve's story, *ipse dixit.* I simply can't help likenesses and differences, *ad infinitum;* no two alike, like a beautiful patchwork quilt made of tiny scraps, to keep my brain warm.

"Did you discover a great new poem every spring, Steve?"

Steve didn't recognize my language; he is as acute as a filly—toward me.

"That's not corny," I explained, "that's Walter Pater."

And a little later when Steve, looking over a seed catalogue, began to talk about, well, he mentioned a hyssop, strangely enough (to *me*, sensitive to suggestion and paraphernalia and whereabouts and my own associative ideas): A hyssop is an aromatic plant. (I wonder if it has both male and female organs, stamen and pistil; at least it has a strange perfume, indicative of itself; what does it *do?* Does it need affection, reach out to you as you pass, respond to your touch? Is it a little trembling floral hermaphrodite? Does it smell like disinfectant with sugar in it?)

"Steve, darling," I said cautiously, "I don't see what men see in each other." And as he did not answer, I said, "Boys, yes and no." The adolescent boy (I thought): he walks on tiptoe and his soul is black as ink; but is it? No, I am antipathetic, quite naturally, I suppose. I am curious but unsympathetic, and Steve isn't helping me to identify myself with two-by-two lads, lost in a limbo I've never glimpsed.

"A young man is fancy," Steve said, looking as if he were gently laughing at my feminine innocence, "I told you I found out it worked."

"Yes, I've finished that part," I said, and I thought, "It is like pure waxen flowers in primary colors growing out of animal excrement."

"Perhaps," I went on to myself, "this is the true spiritual period, the only abstraction, if anything sexually impelled is pure, of his love-life, of a man's love-life. It is unmotivated, isn't it? He wants little, doesn't he? Even in his hydraulic homestead an imperative hunger motivated him; the survival instinct kept him busy, and Ginger's appeal was certainly ambivalent, impure in an almost chemical sense, and the group seizures a reversion to fable. Now we have a tender comradeship, twins of the bosom of maybe a goddess, Diana of the Ephesians, with countless breasts as sweet as meringues. Later, anesthetized, won't it be survival again that he seeks in woman? children? Perpetuation; make sons and daughters? Rebirth; legalized transmigration, love with a purpose; marriage. And after that is accomplished, will Virgo, alias Steve, ever find an equable tenderness again to the one I shall try to tell about? Virgo, as I have said, is the sixth sign; nocturnal, described as "melancholy, earthy, and cold." This hardly seems to me to be descriptive of Steve and whether he will be equal to his astrological fate remains to be seen. I know scarcely more than you, dear reader, at this point. Melancholy can mean most anything; Steve is a bit moody, but how can anyone be earthy and cold, too? One must have patience in these astronomical things. The "duo-decimal division of the belt has outlived all the dubious conclusions that have been drawn from it," so I have been told and whatever it means; and time is measured in eons.

"I was very young and very angry," Byron said of his adolescence; that adolescence, peculiar to him, it is true, that lasted throughout his life, that handsome mama's boy who fled again and again to Greece; and *"in grande ab-bondanza* they let Byron's blood"; his lungs *"gigantiselle,"* and "between the pericardium and the heart there was about an ounce of lymph," his autopsy reads; "the kidneys were very large but healthy, and the *versica* relatively small"; and as an addenda, as revealing as a woman's postscript, "It took two strong men to pull apart his skull which was full of blood." I wonder what they were after in this vicious research; a poem? And I do not know if this passionate pathological instance is a rarity or not, nor what star Byron was born under, nor whether he nursed the countess, his mother. I do know that he could not endure to see a woman he loved, eat, he was so sensitive to that sort of physical reference.

Well, Steve, no poet, takes it easier than that. And he does not know that Atys unmanned himself beneath a pine tree nor why. He simply takes the walk with John that so many boys take. From the beginning of literary history: Castor and Pollux; Romulus and Remus; Julius Caesar and Masintha; Marius and Flavian; Rocky and Butch.

It was John the most admirable who turned to Steve and asked, "Is your homework done?"

"Just about," he replied, and when John added quietly,

"Let's, then, take a walk," it came exactly at the right time for Steve. For a month he had been ready but not aware of what he was ready for. He had outgrown over night the Reds, the Rockys, Butch and Skinny. A big eraser had wiped out the fantastic relationship as cleanly as a little eraser had washed off the school blackboard minor problems in chalk. His slingshot lay untouched in the back of his desk; his ardor was taking a rest. And in this restful, even pleasant, but brand new, state he began to notice things that probably had always been there: colors and sights and sounds; an orchestra in the background tuning up. He had, with help, been making too much of a commotion to hear, had drowned out an aria. So he became aware of John, John the most admirable. He had first noticed him the last day he had come out of the woods with his little eccentrics after a violent and libidinous game called "Pocahontas and John Smith." The light in his eye that made Christina catch her breath was beginning to waver; he felt a slight disgust for the first time, although his crazy embraces with boys and trees had inflamed him as usual; but the anarchy in him, perhaps, if that was it, was retreating. He had had enough. It was ebb tide; the neap. And his dark eyes looked elsewhere. John, whom he'd seen without attention every day at school, although he, John, was a year older, an important year, and two grades ahead of him, was skirting the woods across the tracks with his Irish setter at his heel, a book in one hand;

bareheaded. I have to admit that he was handsome, different. As Steve stood still, a thing of beauty himself, dark, and watchful as a cat, pliable, a stillness in him, gentle, harmony, I can only think of, in his whole body and stance, his former (five minutes ago) grain worshipers, whatever they were, shuffled past him. He stood so still! letting the transformation, I suppose, take place like the little spirit in a carpenter's leveler inside him.

"Steve took a chance in the middle of a trance—boop tee de boop—tee de boop—tee de boop!" they chanted. But Steve didn't hear; he stood, intestate, as it were; all by himself for just that second like that second when Daphne was neither maid nor tree, the middle part of a metamorphosis, it must be wonderful, and came on home alone.

"Mom?"

Christina was ironing. The smell of dampness and heat, fresh laundry, flavored with celery salt was in the room and he noticed it; it was pleasant; outside, on the way home that significant fall day, it had smelled like pineapple and burned toast. Christina put the heavy iron down on the dungarees and the steam mounted to her face; she didn't look up.

"Your supper's in the oven."

Steve felt new, and almost glad he wasn't noticed, as if he had had a haircut, but Christina felt it without looking up. She thought he had hurt himself and she was being calm. Men, even little men, must be brave. Steve told me how he had in some forgotten manner twisted his hand so that it was practically on backwards. He had raised a howl and run into the kitchen, "Mom! Mom! My hand!" Christina had been at the sink and had not turned around then, either. ("The Antiphlogistine is in the cupboard.") She never would, not Christina. But I know the scars and adhesions in the heart these scenes leave, and I feel for Christina. She loved her men and this was Christina's etiquette.

Steve had not asked for anything and so did not miss anything; the question mark after Mom was a tone of voice, a new tone to Christina, and that is why she wondered if he was hurt. As he turned and kneeled to take his supper out of the oven his mother studied him intently for the few seconds she had. She looked at him individually and objectively and relatively. The three older boys trooped through her head. When the comparison was finished and the important similarities and differences noted, allowing for this and that, of course, eliminating some, keeping some; remembering what she had heard and what she had read and discarding most of it, she allowed herself at the end of this maternal scrutiny a half-second, penetrating look at Steve, her Steve, himself, so fixed that he looked up, "Did I forget something, Mom?"

"No, Steve; good-night, Steve," but what Christina really said was, "Good-by forever, Steve." Wasn't it? And

the fragrant mist from one of her men's shirts under her
iron seemed to encircle her; she was, for a moment, invisible, incognito. Where had she gone? Up attic? And how
much of the genie-like behavior of his mom did Steve per-
ceive?

My Hero

———

55

CHAPTER FOUR

"O.K.," Steve had said to John's "Let's, then, take a walk," and they went out of the schoolyard together. Sudden friendships among the boys of Public School No. 9 caused little comment, if any. "Boys," Miss Janeway had said, "are like hop-toads"; she wrinkled up her nose, "you never know which way they'll jump, ugh," and she lifted her skirt as if there was one right there. Behind her back the boys called pretty Miss Janeway "Fluff," and if one of them had, one of a number I can think of had, been right there, he would have made the most of Miss Janeway's skirt gesture. There was hardly a boy who hadn't dreamed of Fluff naked as a twig. One could wonder why she took so much time on her ensembles; or on her, what she called, hair-do, as most of them liked it long and flowing, and as they liked so went their dreams. Their impudence and familiarities knew no bounds and in the telling it got a little ugly. I've no doubt some kept their dreams secret, and a few maybe felt a sublimated sweetness in her real presence next day, but most of them were through with her in an hour; rough lads. I would say "poor Fluff," if I didn't know of a not so honorable attempt on her part to seduce John. John the most admirable. And because John is Steve's dearest it is not a digression to tell about it. It may or may not affect our Steve.

For a little while the new friends walked along in silence. It was three o'clock, neither need be home till six; there was plenty of time.

"I'll pick up Patsy," said John, and stopping by at his house, they left their lunch boxes inside the fence and let out the bounding shining feather-tailed Patsy, the only bitch in town with a pedigree, and belonging to the A.K.C., an equivalent for a dog to membership in the Colonial Dames. Patsy stood up on her hind legs and gave each boy a bony hug and each boy laughed; "Good Dog," they said. From then on they were alone, Patsy reporting back only at intervals, her tongue hanging out further and further, her feathery tail gathering burrs, and her thin sides shining and heaving. She prescribed that triangular course, while the boys went straight ahead, that keeps a dog informed of certain things, only occasionally letting the scent of a rabbit or a squirrel divert her. Then she would return to Steve and John, give them a nearsighted glance to be sure it was they and be off again. The boys, not being girls, felt no need to entertain each other; neither was embarrassed by a silence that lasted an hour. John was the more thoughtful; Steve responded to the woods in a new way as if he had never been there before, and not much of him had, only his body. The shining locust skins clinging to the bark of the trees might have been the old hides of naughty boys who like John are tender and new now. A beastly gesture is all that is left of their former existence.

"What is that?" said Steve kicking up the path at a shiny mixture.

"Mica," said John.

"How did this little sea-shell get here?" said Steve.

"Birds," said John.

"What kind of a tree is that?"

"An oak."

"And that one?"

"A beech; and that's a sugar maple," John volunteered. John was the teacher. Steve learned fast.

The next day without any previous agreement they left the school together and John took Steve on only a slightly different walk, and the next day and the next they contentedly did nothing much, but a big atmosphere was being created by their friendship, an intimate understanding; a very choice something was getting into their blood, almost; something like a eclogue or an elegy was being written in the woods, maybe a requiem.

"Wait! Watch!" said John softly; he was looking into an oak; he put out one hand and laid it against Steve's wrist, "Ssh!" A tiny bird flew out of the tree scattering a few bright leaves. "It's a Least Flycatcher," said John; but

Steve saw no Least Flycatcher; he was looking at John; he felt John's soft finger tips on his unprotected wrist; it was as if he had laid his hand on Steve's sensitive heart. John seemed to feel something and he looked at Steve. Steve was gazing longingly into John's cerulean eyes as if, and that's what they looked like, they were the only pieces of sky in the world and Steve's eyes to John, I suppose, like chocolate-colored velvet, looked the color of the woods itself. A strained expression came into John's face. He knew. An ever so slight coolness came over him, a chill; he had already let go of Steve, as it were, but he also moved away a little; it was only perceptible but Steve felt checked, although he had made no advance. John's company, the daily walks, satisfied him; he was happier than he had ever been; what more could there be or could he ask for? But he felt hurt and John uneasy.

"What are you reading?" asked John a little later.

"Oh, I'm not reading anything," said Steve, "why?"

"Let's go to the library tomorrow if it rains."

"Yes," said Steve, "I'd like to; if it rains but not if it doesn't; I don't want to, unless you do. If it rains, O.K."

At home Steve was beginning to look like Cinderella and his big brothers, like that one's elder sisters, sneered a little at his new look. Did they recognize it? Their walks were over. They teased him; they wanted to muss him up; he had a loneness about him and a beauty, an innocence, that irritated them, and as they couldn't say ugly things in front of Christina they indulged in references and anecdotes with double meanings, watching Steve for a tell-tale flush. But Steve, like a girl, even more so than a girl, less sophisticated than girls are just plain born, seemed to have a protective ectoplasm about him, impervious to evil. His mother, not too much fooled by her big boys' tricky talk, was a little bit fooled by her youngest son's silences. He was so completely independent, seemed so competent; a boy with no needs. He certainly had no need of her. She turned to Anna who was pompously mothering her doll. "Go to bed, Anna," she said crossly.

It looks as if I were leaving out Sam and I am. Sam isn't necessary to my story just now nor to the others at this time. Anna did hesitate and glance at him before trotting off to bed, and I think he gave her an understanding glance, a little apologetic. "It is early but let's not cross your mother," it seemed to say.

The telephone! and it looked like every male, with the exception of Steve, started. Even Sam whom we aren't talking about looked sideways. The other little men could have had names like funnypaper talk written in balloons over their heads; "Sally," "Jane," "Phoebe."

Christina called from the kitchen, "Steve, John."

As Steve started toward the door one of the boys put out his foot as if to trip him but Steve easily avoided it. Eddie, eighteen months older than Steve, got to the phone first and in a silly girlish voice said, "Oh Johnnie, this is Stevie," but his hand was over the mouthpiece; it was for the benefit of his brothers. As he handed the receiver to Steve, in the privacy of the kitchen, he made a gesture; well, he curved his hand over his groin and drew in his breath sharply between his teeth. If Steve got the idea of Eddie's suggestive and indecent pantomime he did not show it in any way at all.

"I can't go walking with you, Steve, tomorrow; Father Gulick asked me to go fishing and mother says I should."

"Oh John!"

Pause.

"Steve?"

"Yes, it's me."

"I said I . . . ."

"O.K.," said Steve bravely; he felt as if he had received a blow; his future seemed to disappear and his eyes filled with tears, "O.K., John . . . . and . . . Wednesday?" he asked shyly.

"Yes, Wednesday, definitely. So long."

"So long."

Steve went up the back stairs and stood looking out into the night that had become ominous. He was looking into his first sorrow, his first real disappointment, and it seemed to have an everlastingness about it. Wednesday? He got hold of himself, and the night, the next day, passed.

Miss Janeway rapped on her desk, "Steve, pay attention! Do you or don't you know the date of the French and Indian War?"

"I don't."

"Maybe John will tell you this afternoon," she said
meanly, and the class snickered. But they weren't just
snickering at Steve. The whole thing had a delicious
double meaning: It only took one boy to have seen something between Fluff and John for all the rest to enjoy it,
and they knew Steve was catching it, not so much for not
knowing the answer, but because she didn't. She hadn't
been able to make John. He had turned her down! Philip
Fraser, a little boy without much prestige, not a member
of anything, sandy-haired with an in-betweenness about
him, neither male nor female, attracting no one, was fortunate enough to have overheard the rebuff, and whether
he made up the rest, he can hardly be blamed if he did,
considering his new popularity and he liked it, I don't
know.

"Tell it again, Phil."

"I just said I heard her, they were in the hall, you all
had gone. She said, 'Johnny, please.'"

"Johnny please," they mimicked.

"He said, 'I'm sorry, Miss Janeway, I'm going with Steve
this afternoon,' and she said, 'Oh Johnny.'"

"Oh Johnny."

"And she said, 'Don't you like me, aren't I pretty?'"

It is hard to say what really happened because Philip
wasn't very bright and not very imaginative, but the boys,
after hearing of Fluff's indiscretion, showed signs of impudence and familiarity that used to be confined to their

dreams, and they callously divided her body and charms amongst each other in their conversations and imaginings as if she were aggies. Then certain plans were made and boys drew lots; and one Perkins, sixteen and big for his age, was coached to stay late on a certain afternoon and see if he could get to kiss Fluff. It had to be on the mouth. But when he met the group afterwards as had been agreed, he boasted that it was easy, he had felt her breasts and put his hand under her skirt, and she had agreed to meet him later in the boat house by the pond and let him do it. It was said there were witnesses that night who later enjoyed Fluff, too, and that enthusiasm ran high. Philip overheard some salacious reminiscences and found a note to Fluff that didn't mince descriptive words, thanking her for a "hot good time," and being a nasty little boy with no hope of sharing Fluff and no longer necessary to the boys, he told his mother. Fluff left on the 8:05 that night and after an unexplained holiday the boys found themselves under the tutelage of a big strapping female who looked what a policewoman is supposed to look like. Instead of Quelques-fleurs the room smelled of good clean soap. Who knows what really happened? I only know Philip's mother, who was on the Board of Regents, and thin lipped, said, "She proved undesirable." Well, maybe. You see I did a little research but too many years had passed, too many seasons with other problems, hard times and better times; and didn't they all want to forget? Now that this one and that one was holding down a good job,

the other had a nice family of well-bred girls and so-and-so
was in the government? And maybe Fluff was in just one
old watch. I hope so.

But it wasn't so hard to find out more about John because his mother loved to talk of him. You see he was dead
and had been her only child. "My boy was too good for
this world." And, "I was spared anyway losing him maybe
in the war," she said.

But we must get back to John's and Steve's walk the
afternoon of the day that John turned down Fluff and
Philip heard it, setting off a startling chain-reaction of
criminal behavior and bawdy counterpoint that chills the
heart, because I've no doubt, pretty and frivolous Miss
Janeway responded to Perkins, might not have otherwise,
because of the loss, almost, of her feminine identity upon
being repulsed by John. Hence the pyramids. She might
not have reacted so bestially if she had known that John's
tastes were what they were and that she was really just as
desirable as before his snub. But she got out of town too
fast to know what causes certain things. She had to. And
she will not return to our history of bad boys. I'm glad
for Steve's sake. I can't promise he would not have fallen.
Miss Janeway was a kind of—shop-lifter is all I can think
of—and a type as old as the hills, primordial; she had a
kind of sophistication, but she was disarming, too. Maybe
that baby-talk plus two years in Teachers High, plus you
know what . . . . Well that really is all. So long, Fluff.

(And while I am writing this, of course, I see and talk to

Steve, but I do not show him what I write; it is to be a surprise, the story of his life; this part, perhaps, based on his remark, "A young man is fancy." He did say yesterday, "There's a fungus on the rye.")

Steve is happy as they start out and John as happy as that young man with a past and no future can be. That John is dead as I write this makes it harder for me than him. Steve is almost happier than as if John's day off (from him) with Father Gulick hadn't made him feel an almost intuitive despair yesterday. There is no doubt John loved Steve, as Steve really loved, to idolatry, John. But Steve's appeal was almost womanish and it frightened John; it suggested abandon, and giving up something it had taken a long time to get a leg on, as it were, a kind of abstract intellectual, nearly cerebral, love which he thought divine, and I do not use the word lightly. Steve's divinity was as good as his, a purity of intensity, a desire without preoccupation, as the crow flies; and he was not afraid. Perhaps the difference in their innocence will become clear when I tell you what John's mother told me, and what I learned from her that she did not tell me; but in the meantime let us go on: Steve, happy, lost his shyness, felt nearly equal, in good spirits, uninhibited now as his friend had been, and slid his warm paw into John's long cool hand. John leaned over and kissed him, a clear cool kiss, and linked his arm to Steve's. Steve was no happier than he expected to be. There was no doubt in his mind about anything; he could have answered any question on any exam. What a moment that we have all felt! But not very often.

"We are going to the river bank, Marius," said John.

"Yes," said Steve.

"I called you 'Marius.'"

"You said we were going to the river bank."

"You have never heard of Marius and Flavian?"

"It doesn't matter."

"We love each other dearly."

"Yes I know."

"We will soon be there."

The river wasn't exactly a river, a small stream fresh and bright at this time of year after much rain but usually just Johnson's Crick, and there was a bank and the sun shone on it; a warm November three o'clock day. John gently lay Steve down and embraced him, "I want to teach you everything," he said, "because . . ."

Steve felt a book under his back, "What is this?" He was lying on a breviary, black with a gold cross embossed on it, and he put it aside waiting for, I suppose, felicity. But he saw John's face; it looked inspired but he, Steve, was left out of it. A terrible jealousy bigger than he was, older than he was, without content, melted his insides. His cheeks glowed. John misunderstood and had no difficulty seducing, without staining himself in Steve's eyes, Steve. So soon after "tragedy" again was Steve divinely happy. And then John, one arm cradling the beloved dark head of his first student, the little passionate neophyte, our darling Steve, told him stories; taught him in an afternoon almost all he knew, and it was Greek. John's hours with Father Gulick had been well spent, he was indoctrinated and longed to indoctrinate. And Plato's name was like a rainbow in the sky. As long as John caressed him Steve listened, but to his voice more than his words. ". . . that their progeny is lovelier and more endearing than ordinary parents." ". . . that the 'teacher' is the lover with a desire to conceive and produce together with the object of his love whose image is never divided from his mind."

"I love you!" Steve cried out in a voice that breaks my heart.

"Consider the immortality of great poets, my little Steve-Marius; isn't it better than other ordinary people's children? We are immortal." And he added unpoetically and bitterly, "Women!" And then softly, "Sluts!"

I wish I did not have to quote this boy, so soon to be dead, like this, but it affects Steve's nerves and Steve is the one. He longs for a terrible affection to the point of oblivion, and I suppose the reason none of this bitterness of John's ever became apparent in Steve as long as I have known him was purely physical. His was the stronger primary appeal and John stopped talking, himself seduced; and they played until they fell asleep; Steve the teacher. But on the way home, sane again, still adoring, he looked up shyly at the fair Flavian as he discoursed on Elysium and when they separated John put in his hand Plato's

Symposium on love, which I don't think Steve ever has read; and he never knew, even after John's death, why he had called him Marius, not having read Walter Pater either. But I have, and John died of the plague as surely as Flavian did, for a Greek reason.

There were other walks. Our two lads went through the woods amidst an *éclat* of leaves, Patsy weaving through the backdrop of young birches, and heeling them home. When they rested or lay on the river bank again in the Spring, Patsy tore up the tender, light green grass, emetic, and yawning and retching, smiling when it was over, had a pleasant afternoon, too.

"To heel! Patsy!"

"Yes *sir*!"

Toward the end, that I know of but they didn't, of these peripatetics, which means the philosophical wanderings of, I suppose, philosophers (they were, weren't they, heirs of that Socrates who along with wisdom dispensed a sugar-coated pill: the act of love, a symbol of oneness, the thesis: I love you?), well, toward the end of these wanderings Steve began to do a little talking himself, the result, perhaps, of a creative act, which cannot be barren. "I want to be," he said in parenthesis, but he began to talk about objects, things, parts of things; a beautiful machine was forming in his mind, complicated and thrillingly functional.

"John?"

"Marius?"

“Percussion is wonderful, that is what I am thinking about.”

“What is percussion?” asked John.

“It is shock produced by collision: Everything like that is what you begin with; then . . .”

It sounds, I know, as if Steve had been hanging around Sam’s garage and I suppose he had been, a little, but to me it looks as if the act of love had reminded him of an older ambition than a choice of profession. There had been an earlier shock, another near, at least, collision: The train! Was he going to master it in a new way? And at the same time master Christina? All in secret, a big secret, neither himself or Christina to know? Well, anyway, Steve and John, lip to lip, as it were, talked; John of poetry, love, ethics, the science of moral duty, and Steve, of engines.

CHAPTER FIVE

As I said, I learned from John's mother quite a lot about him. After his death her tongue was loosened and she was glad to have me to talk to. Father Gulick was often there. He was an Anglican priest, Church of England, without much of a flock and a church still to be collected. I did not like him. He was a comforter of women and a seducer of boys, that I felt sure of. He was the kind of snob you want to slap in the face. He was ersatz, a plastic, he quoted the uncontroversial, admired the acceptable, knew an etching from a drypoint, vichyssoise from potato soup. He preferred to sleep between linen sheets even in winter, and liked a green mint frappé after coffee. He affected a miserable, what he thought was a British, accent, and he spoke of Brown's Hotel in London and the head-waiter's attention to him there. I believe he was on that list of those specially acceptable guests who received a plum-cake at Christmas, good Lord! from that fine middle-class establishment. But John's mother admired him, imagined, I suppose, that he was the real thing, a gentleman, and she gave him her best cordials, her best worn linen sheets. She gave him also, unwittingly, John. John's photograph soon was added to the others on the walls of Father Gulick's study, all of them widows' sons; Father Gulick was afraid of papas. He is the only loathsome character in this story and I wish that I could personally unfrock him, expose him mercilessly. In the name of the Father, and the Son, and the Holy Ghost, he fattened himself, the nasty thing, on the white flesh of boys without fathers. Amen.

"Come in!"

I interrupted a game of chess between John's mother and Father Gulick and I heard all about the rare china tea that he was being served. He gave John's mother a French kiss (a touch on either cheek) and left at just the proper interval after I sat down. "*A bientôt,*" he said and gathered up his skirts and left.

I learned that as a little boy, certainly old enough to talk, John was speechless. He was eight years old, intelligent, it seemed, healthy, but no one could get him to speak. Then one day the kerosene stove exploded right behind him and John let out a long complicated compound sentence in a nicely modulated voice. I have no idea what this is indicative of, I simply give it as part of John, who was part of Steve, who is part of me.

I learned that soon afterwards he began writing verses, and the little smudged examples I was shown were certainly just as good as "To a Fringed Gentian" and "Farewell of a Virginia Slave Mother."

"At least I warned him against women," she said unexpectedly, "I could not do it myself and as he had no father I asked Father Gulick; such a gentleman and so fond of John."

"That parvenu with his *paternosters!*" was all I could think of to sputter to myself, but it sounds disgusting, evil, doesn't it?

Although she talked for two hours the above was the only salient prelude, as it were, to suicide that I could glean from the monologue, and as I walked home I didn't think my eavesdropping had given me very much to go on. It looked as if John the most admirable had just grown up against the tide, as it were; he didn't have a chance; at least he did not choose to struggle; he was just washed up on the beach and left there. But violence? Self-destruction? Nonsense! What sort of language is that to use about the sleepy demise of a fairheaded cerulean-eyed boy-poet? *Dolce far niente:* sweet-doing-nothing, it means, and John had found enough of his mother's sedatives to put him to sleep, to do nothing sweetly . . . forever. *Dolce-dolce;* or to change it into Latin, *dulce, dulce et decorum:* sweet and honorable.

"Flavian lay there with the enemy at his breast . . . rare Paestum roses, and the like—procured by Marius for his solace . . . and would at intervals return to labor at his verses . . . while Marius sat and wrote at his dictation, one of the . . . but not poorest specimens of genuine Latin poetry. It was in fact a kind of nuptial hymn . . . celebrated the preliminary pairing and mating together of all fresh things, in the hot and genial spring-time—the immemorial nuptials of the soul of spring itself and the brown earth; and was full of a delighted, mystic sense of what passed between them in that fantastic marriage."

And so John fell upon his sword and the above quotation from Walter Pater, *Marius the Epicurean,* is better than I can do for my Flavian and my Marius: John and Steve. The little epicurean Flavian (and John one and the same) is dead; a pagan end it was called.

And Patsy, the bitch, at his death, shudders and faints; her lips drawn back showing a beautiful set of shiny white teeth; her legs gathered together like the handle of a basket; her tail limp as wet feathers. If only John could be revived as Patsy was with a silver pitcher of cold water! Without so much as a where-am-I she leaped to her feet and fawning and teasing tried to talk, "Yip! Yip!" A powerful blackout saved her from knowing her loss; she doesn't to this day remember a thing, and she shines in the sun like a red flame. She sniffs at every pair of boy's legs, and she often goes to the river-bank where she lies warming her stomach on the earth and snapping absent-mindedly at gnats; and she lopes home nose down, to heel, starting and slowing up and waiting a moment and wagging her tail; sitting down hard and panting, a big

grin on her face. She eats well; she doesn't remember a
thing.

Steve acted, although he did not faint, did not seem to
be mercifully anesthetized, in much the same way. He
walked in the woods, a rehearsal, it seemed, of the past:
the same mica underfoot; the oak, the beech, the sugar
maple; the Least Flycatcher darted out of the same tree,
scattering the same bright leaves; but he was thinking of
the engine, the cool bright and shining parts of a beautiful
performance; motion, a deliberate assembly. Long ago he
had conquered, hadn't he, anger and hatred and fear? . . .
but the night of John's death he dreamed a divine dream.
Christina, who had suffered in her boy's place all night,
imagining his grief, did not know whether to be angry or
relieved to see that look on Steve's face and that soft and
prowling, harmonious gait. "Is he cold?" "Is he heartless?"
at such a time . . . to . . .? she thought. Didn't she know
what a good teacher she had been? What a noble enemy
she had been; what a victorious retreat, let's call it planned withdrawal, was Steve's?

The Anglican managed everything in the best taste, of
course, and the service, so beautiful, solaced the bereaved,
and a thin-stemmed glass of green chartreuse, Father
Gulick. And we all slept better, I must admit, when himself "managed" a handful of deacons, and John's body, his
spirit having broken the law, was not dumped out back
with the witches and necromancers but laid to its final rest

in consecrated ground, next his scanty kinfolk. It seems
that Father Gulick, not content to keep his hands off
John, even dead, had performed what his mother called
"a lovely ceremony." He had re-baptized John, after his
sinful and illegal act, in holy water as cool as the boy's
forehead, and had given him communion: a few drops of
that green chartreuse between the sweet slightly open lips
(he had looked like an angel taking his first breath of
rarified air), and crumbs of almond cake from Huntley
& Palmer. Only the incense was missing and Father Gulick
had not, evidently, "managed" to get a cloud to open or a
dove to sit on the window sill. But the widowed, childless
one now was very grateful and forgave herself a lot of
things, as did Father Gulick as he heard her confession.
Pax vobiscum.

CHAPTER SIX

I have been long gone, I am afraid, living the thrilling little lives of two saints, kept from becoming almost sentimental about my archives, saved from an ivory tower pink with fable, by realistically frustrating characters— for instance: Gulick and Fluff—weak and fuzzy ones like John's mother and Philip Fraser; and it's time I took a look at Steve, grown up, before I go on, backwards I mean, with himself while he grew up. A few nights ago Steve dreamed. A deep and healthy sleeper, he seldom does, and that, I suppose, is why he spoke of it at all.

"I don't get it," said Steve.

"What?"

"It doesn't make sense but it has happened before; why should I dream about a woman I hardly know? even dislike?"

"What (but I knew) did you dream about her?"

"Well, I did it to her—good; I don't get it."

My heart missed a beat, I was jealous, but that didn't

account for the tachycardia. You will see why, as a writer, working only with hints, dealing with a man who is taciturn, not interested in his or anybody else's past, a man of today, who believes in taking what comes as it may and not worrying about why and what or the reasons for, I am thrilled. I asked him the next question knowing the answer before he told me but not asking him right away.

"It seems strange but that is often what happens," I said. "I imagine you don't dislike the one you dream of as much as you think. Perhaps she seems repulsive to you in the daytime but repulsion and appeal are so close, and in sleep your choice, your will, is dissolved. Or, on the contrary, you want really to do it—good—to, for instance, your fiancée, let us say, and your dream, your unconsciousness, protects you, oddly enough, from this sin in your own eyes and you exonerate yourself by doing it to someone you do not respect and so feel no evil; only as you wake up are you disgusted and even then a little sentiment for the ravished one, ugly or not, stays with you a short while, and if you see her on the bus she is somehow a little closer, less ugly . . . no?"

"No," agreed Steve. "The funny thing is," he went on, interrupting, and I don't blame him, as I started to elucidate some more, "It's usually . . . with me . . . , well . . . it follows, and I'm ashamed, tragedy!"

"Oh, Steve, you are wonderful," I thought to myself, "tell me, tell me."

"Tell me what you mean," I said out loud, calmly.

“I . . .”

“Yes?”

“I want to, I mean I used to want to, and well, I did do it all by myself after my best friend died. It was the first real tragedy in my life because I loved him. But after the funeral—well, I did it.”

I put my arms around Steve and kissed him. He had given me confidence in myself as an artist which is almost as important as being confident as a woman which thanks to my lover I had been for some time.

“Shall we?” he said, and I neglected my work.

“You know I forgot to tell you,” said Steve, as if his mind was dissatisfied, perhaps, with my explanation the other night re dreams of fair and ugly, too, women— “You know that night it blew up a gale and the tide was so high and storm signals . . .”

“Were up from Cape Hatteras to Block Island?” I finished for him.

“Yes. Well, I didn’t see you for a few days, remember?”

“What happened?”

“I nearly got killed.”

“Steve! Why didn’t you tell me?”

“Why, afterwards I forgot, I suppose.”

“Well?”

“I was out of cigarettes and I took the car to that little tavern close to. I left it outside and went in. I was soaking wet and I ordered a drink. In the middle of my drink, the wind was a good sixty miles an hour, I heard a squeal of wind, a splintering, and a crash—slow—like. A big pine had fallen smack on my car. It scared me to look at it."

It didn't sound like Steve to be scared or even bother to tell a story of what might have been. What else was there?

"Suze?"

"Yes?"

"I hate to tell you but I wanted to do it—good." He laughed. "To the girl behind the bar! It was a strong desire. I could have raped her! And I don't like her! She's no girl either, she's the wife of one of the neighbors with a face like a dish of pabulum."

"Steve, darling, was that the day before your dream?" (This was the question I had planned to ask, knowing the answer—but.)

"Why, yes."

"Will you please tell me why you can't figure that one out for yourself then?"

"I just didn't, that's all."

"Did she remind you in any way of your mother?" (I blush at this old stuff, dear reader.)

"Hell no!"

And of course she didn't, that would be too simple. But I felt I should have the neighbor's wife moved away. I felt that there must be a prohibitive attraction there and so

close to Steve! just a few steps, a path, a doorway . . . and
a divine dream! I hate it! and put it out of my mind. I
don't like this part of my story.

"Suze?"

"Let's not talk about it any more."

"But you want me to talk!"

"Not about *her*."

"Oh, Suze, don't be like that, you should see her, she . . ."

"Shut up!"

"Have it your way, but I never would have told you,
it's a pretty bad thing, not dreaming, but how I feel after
a tragedy and what I have done; I never would have mentioned it, ever, to anyone. I used to wonder if anybody
ever felt and did what I did, before, but I didn't like to
ask; maybe I was different, queer; but you seem to know
things ahead of time, almost before they happen. How
come? I feel I'm not telling you anything new and because
you *know* you can't be shocked or surprised, even. You
do know, don't you?"

"I don't *know* anything; I make things up and people
tell me about them later." (This was the absolute truth.)

And so this chapter closes with an aesthetic question,
or is it a question of magic? I am an alumna of the occult,
you remember; and do you know why much bigger
and handsomer and funnier males than you (among my
readers) used, on islands and in jungles, to take off their
hats, or feathers, to women? get up when they came into
the hut? take their pipes, or whatever, out of their mouths

when they met her on the path? step aside? bow? It was the mystery! And they were mighty scared and respectful. Why did women bleed in time with the moon, for instance, and what was the cause of pregnancy? Those were the days! And still are, I understand, in far-away places. Bless their hearts; big black men in far-away places!

"Steve, darling, did you know that in some tribes it is very taboo to stay alone with your mother-in-law?"

"It's O.K. with me," said Steve.

"It is punishable by death!"

My Hero

CHAPTER SEVEN

The French have a nice saying, *"Revenons à nos moutons"*: Let us return to our sheep. Well, let us return to my lamb, who is Steve. It seems that I have become very attached to my lamb and I hope this literary adoption of him turns out all right. It was harder, as I suggested in the beginning, for me to pass through his adolescence than apparently it was for him. My antipathy I have written away and I think now of Novalis, the mystic seeker after "the blue flower"; the scarlet anemone that sprang from the blood of Adonis: Anemone means, at least it, in turn, springs from, *Naaman,* meaning Darling, darling being an epithet of Adonis.

"Darling."

"What? Now what are you thinking about; you think too much."

"I'm eavesdropping on your heart, dear," I said. I laid my ear against his chest and heard it, its big generous beat and a slight whirring sound like a fan, and my own heart beating against my own ear and from another part of the house I heard the icebox automatically shut off; I even thought I heard a ticking in the telephone wires and a murmur in the lamp. "It's like a machine shop in here," I said.

"Harmonization and adjustment," I added, "like a kind of truth; a grown-up truth in this world. And it works!"

"Now you're beyond me."

"And myself, too. I wish I did not have to leave you, Steve, as a boy, I mean, and have you grow up. You were sweet."

"I was a stinker."

I shook my head. "Now for two years you worked in your father's garage; isn't that what you did?"

"Yes, I did."

"Well, tell me a little."

Steve's eyes began to shine. "At first it was electricity."

Well, he told me and I listened, enthralled, and amazed and enraptured, and almost jealous, as Steve spoke of "the machine" as I thought men only talked of beautiful women. He told me about the "Delta," the "Star," and the "Open-Delta," each a "method of Connection" and I thought (how could I help it?), lying beside him, that he was indeed speaking of the act of love, and its thrilling variables. Hadn't we experimented together.

"There is a coziness for different angles . . ."

"Yes, I know," I murmured into his coat, . . . "I want you Steve. . . ."

"I thought you wanted to hear about electricity and motors. What do you mean you know? Do you?"

"Coziness; yes, I know about that."

"The cosine of the angle of lag is equal to the power factor."

"Oh, *that* kind of coziness!"

"There is no other kind!"

He really meant it. That's what he was talking about, wasn't it? And I felt ashamed of my almost perverted, really, disassociation of things; but not wanting to let go of the pretty images in my mind I said, "Angles I know about and methods of connection, too. Please Steve! I know; I'll show you. You don't know *everything*."

But Steve, usually so warm, so eager and generous with his love-making, was talking about, I felt, another woman and giving her his undivided attention. I cooled a little and said to myself, "You asked for it, now listen." But what is a Star? A Delta? An Open-Delta? When he speaks of these in that caressing voice, his eyes deep and dark, gesticulating fondly with his hands, aren't they parts, dearest and thrilling parts, of a beloved body? and no boy's body now, hesitant, doubtful, but the real thing. Yes, that's what it is that he is talking about so tenderly, a thing, the machine.

"It is so clean!" he said as my mind began to wander, and I looked up. I looked at him closely, as I imagine Christina used to look when the woman in her was baffled. That's the way she stared at him when he came home from his metamorphosis, after the *fauni* and before Flavian. There was a fine purity of intention and attention about him now, too, and I think, "I am the animal, he is the angel." Well, for the present anyway. But I see what he means, "clean." At the same time I see the boy in the machine shop, in coveralls spotted and slippery with grease and oil. I see Callahan and Claude, the master mechanics in Sam's garage, black as savages, only their clear blue eyes making them look as if they wore masks at a ball. Nevertheless, out of it comes a clean thing, the machine, pure and shining, desirable; abstract in the sense that all waste in time and space has been eliminated; vigorous, functional, ductile, virile, and chaste; resonant. No wonder Callahan and Claude and Steve drop their tools and stand in a kind of catalepsy, like bridesmaids around the bride, in ecstatic admiration when she begins to hum. Steve interrupted my lovely picture of two men and a boy adoring the beautiful Thing.

"The Hillman Minx," he said admiringly, "did you ever get a good look at the front axle of the Minx?"

"Well, no, not actually a good look. What did you say her name was?"

"Minx, but other manufacturers here, too, use a rigid radius rod universally jointed at each end."

"They do?"

"There's a more elaborate scheme sometimes employed: the radius rod forms the arm of the front-axle hydraulic shock absorber, a spring-loaded ball joint being provided

to absorb any shock set up by the sudden application of
the brakes."

"Oh brakes! She's got brakes?"

"Yes, the brake drum is placed within the dished wheel
to reduce the angle of inclination of the wheel and swivel-
pin."

"Well, yes but . . ."

"As the rear brake band is applied," Steve made a sweet
gesture, "the rear drum is locked," he clenched his fist
gently and surely, "and the first rear internal gear is held
stationary . . . so."

"Ahh," I said.

"Consequently, rotation of the front sun gear forces a
first set of planet gears to walk around with the sun gear."

"To *walk around* with who!" I interrupted incredu-
lously.

"With the sun gear, but at a further reduction."

"Oh, I see."

"As the carrier for these planet gears is integral," Steve
folded his hands together, "with the internal gear of the
second rear epicyclic, the rotation of this internal gear
at a speed lower than that of the second sun gear causes
the planet gears of the second epicyclic to rotate at an
intermediate reduction of two point two six to one in the
rear unit."

"Gosh!"

"The total gear reduction of the gear box is therefore
the reduction of the front epicyclic train multiplied by

that of the rear unit. This is one point four four to one,
times two point two six to one, which equals three point
two five four to one."

"Steve?"

"But you ought to see, if you never have, a cut-away
exhibition chassis. Look, I have a photograph here in my
wallet; isn't she sweet? It shows the four point rubber
mounting, too, used to support the power unit of a ten-h.p.
Ford Prefect."

"And in his watch," I thought, "what do you suppose
he has in there, 'an independent rear suspension'?"

"Steve, dear, you loved it, didn't you?"

"I was happy."

"Didn't you have a girl friend?"

Steve went on as if I had not spoken, "I had to find
out," he said.

"What?" I said.

"How it worked."

"But you did."

"Yes," he said, ignoring my reference. "I don't understand how people can look at a clock and not want to find
out how it works, or a stove; they light a stove, but they
don't know how or why it lights!" He looked at me lovingly as if he did not include me in this stupid incredible
lot of dopes.

For two years Steve spent his days and part of his nights
with "her" then.

"You and your Minx!" I said teasingly, but I caught his

enthusiasm, if not his single-mindedness. "It was a straight cerebral thrill with no skirts on it," I said to myself. I felt how he must have felt. I felt how Callahan and Claude felt initiating him, showing him how, "Easy does it"; whispering of magnetos, and torque; spark plugs and shock absorbers; valves, visibility, rack-and-pinion; liquamatic drive, ignition, compensation and dynamos. And then with a shop full of parts, new boxes of bolts, nuts, washers, nails and screws, how he put her together from scratch! The right bolt, the right washer, the right nut; as a writer chooses words, a painter, colors; tense, trembling with suspense, but with steady nerve and hand he makes her sing! That is the only way I can describe the lover of engines. She will surely sing; you must capture her attention, too; don't let her mind or senses, whatever the parallel is of an engine being assembled to a mistress being fondled, waver. Concentrate on her; make her happy; and she'll sing. She's really yours; you did it. Without you she does not, cannot, exist, and you know every measurement and weight and level in her; her very pistons gleam, and tremble for your hands. Listen to her hum. She's as clean and thrilling as light, as ardent as a knife; her pitch is true. Take care of her. . . . (How easily I am converted to anything Steve cares about!)

So how could I ask him of girl friends! Those same little hoydens he used to avoid merely grown bigger, that's all, swelled out in front and behind and stretched up, and down too; and hasn't Dodo got a slight squint? Bubbles lumpy calves? and Pinky no breasts? Odious comparisons when you think of what I see reflected in Steve's eyes. It isn't the square panes of glass in the skylight of the garage, alone; pretty as that is, like geometry.

Well, Steve the boy, is happy; he is living in the present, a short present, a present, let us call it, an anonymous gift, that most of us miss. But Steve has got, it appears, a guardian angel. Doesn't she sleep with him? And her influence pervades, in a way, his waking hours. Nothing too awful will happen to Steve. The "fantastic marriage" that might have been binding, with John, has been annulled. It's as if certain love-letters had been burned, evidence destroyed; the *corpus,* or foundation, *delicti,* or offense, removed, and Steve is presented with a new set of instruments to find out how they work.

And so with a megger he learns to measure high resistance and with an ohmmeter he learns about a resistance where accuracy of about one-quarter of one per cent is satisfactory. And Callahan and Claude hover, as if he were the child of their union, over him. They tenderly cleanse his hands of grease with fluffy waste; mend the zipper on his coveralls, sing out, "Watch out sonny for your ding-dong," as they zip him up the front. "Now, then, here's your gimmick, get going; easy does it."

"My father threw a wrench at me," said Steve.
"What!"

Lost in the boy's own concentration; the sing-song and busyness and throbbing of the garage in my ears; the loving care of Callahan and Claude soothing me; it was as if I felt and heard the wrench whiz past my own skull. I put my fingers to my temple and looked at them—blood? I was shocked, but too well acquainted now with my characters to need to ask for details.

Who knows, even Sam, what impossible pressure, what series of frustrations, which ancestor, had made Sam lose his temper and, without taking aim, hurl a wrench at Steve. Wouldn't it have been more sensible to tear the soft legs of the widow out of their sockets, slap Christina's face and throw her mitre in the toilet; accident prone, slither his car into a ditch, rape his Anna, spit in the pulpit of Trinity Church? Why didn't the walk from his home where, it is true, dinner was just a little bit late, calm him?

"Steve's still at the shop," Christina had said without turning from the stove, "and dinner will be a little bit late." Anna stood beside her mother, her thumb in her mouth and one hand high up between her legs, an innocent rapt look on her face. It was as if Sam was giving everybody one last chance; he was in search of the last straw. "Come and kiss daddy, Anna," he said. But Anna heard nothing, saw nothing; she was in some kind of child's heaven, that limbo just around the corner that children go into at no particular time and look like angels while they aren't where they are. Sam turned and was off, his veins swelling, an impotent fury as regular as a woman's menstruation building up in him a dangerous frontal fog, pink, as if there was blood in it.

He opened the sliding doors of the garage softly, seeming to save his strength, and saw Steve.

"Take your thumb out of your mouth, you little tart!"

Steve, it is true, must have resembled Anna sucking her thumb, fondling herself. But just as she might have ducked instinctively, Steve, without turning, curved his body away before the wrench had described a like arc through the air. He felt it fan his cheek. He gently turned a switch and waited until the engine came to a coughing stop, vibrated and was quiet, you could have heard an eccentric pin drop. He wiped a drop of sweat from one of the cylinder heads and picked up his tools.

"I quit," he said, and everyone knew he had.

.

Steve trembled as he walked home. He had picked up a small piece of waste and he methodically wiped his hands that were already free of grease. But he wiped them as Lady Macbeth did, I suppose, to get rid of murder, to cleanse them of blood. He did not in the least lose control of himself; he was used to violence and it really shied off him as if he were armored; a kind of immunity had grown up in him. If he wished to violate his mother and behead his father he was not aware of it in words, neither did his lips form a like dirty phrase as it had when the train had just spared him: "Lick my shit." But the insult of violence shook him to his roots and he could not help, hardly noticed, a stirring between his legs. It was as if that part of him wished to defend him; battle for him without his permission, an involuntary brotherhood; his senses were not affected. He looked down at himself in a kind of innocent astonishment and detachment but did not touch himself, gave himself no comfort. And as if he had sent orders on high, canceling an engagement, his guardian angel did not visit him that night. Man's estate was just around the corner, or up one flight and to your left, and he was on his own.

As he entered the house, Anna rushed at him and embraced his legs and for some reason shouted, "Me! Me! Me! Me, Stevie, Me!" This was unlike Anna who usually eyed Steve from her corner, or anything that she wanted, obliquely. Christina, surprised, turned around but did not see that Steve was any different. It had taken a very young girl to see that Steve was ready for love of a woman. Steve didn't even know it himself.

"Get off me, Anna," but he smiled and caressed her neck.

CHAPTER EIGHT

"If thou fix thy heart on one alone, thou must lose thy senses; a love of one, and one alone, makes mad." This is from "The Alexandrian Erotic Fragment," by Parthenius, and I quoted it to Steve when he told me a little, you know how little, about this part of his life that I am going to try and tell about.

"She was the kind of woman you want to put a mustache on," he said as if that was all there was to it. He was speaking of Augusta's mother, the woman who didn't want him for a son-in-law.

"She was what you call a woman of action; if she saw the dog dead asleep in the hall, his nose under the radiator, with no harm in him, she thought it was time for him to go out. 'Out! Out!' she would say." Steve kicked at the rug, still angry it seemed, although the woman he was speaking of had been dead ten years and Augusta . . . who knows where and what Augusta is. That weak and pretty girl who loved Steve but didn't love him enough and didn't know really what she wanted. But Mrs. Hooker! She did, and she didn't want, not for keeps anyway, Steve. She wanted one of those other lads who stood up when she came in the room.

"I wouldn't stand up for her," said Steve, "I just sat there. Why should I?"

"And did Augusta marry one of the others?"

"No," said Steve, "she married a working man after all and he left her with five children."

"Tell me about Augusta."

"Mrs. Hooker . . ." he began.

"No, Augusta."

"Her mother . . ."

What sort of power, I thought, had old Mrs. Hooker that she animated Steve after all these years, when Augusta, whom he had loved, whom he had caressed— "I had intercourse with her for three years," he had said, to satisfy me, thinking that was all I wanted to know—seemed to have faded out of his memory. He wasn't deliberately keeping anything back. He didn't have any trouble describing Ginger! or that blonde one who asked him outright to come home with her and told him in detail what they would do, "something different"; or any of the other of the women with whom he exchanged favors later on in that period when he got used to sex, the realistic period, when it meant nothing to him at all, any more than going to the movies or three meals a day. "I harmed no one," he said. His girl's mother seemed to have poured ink over an old photo; I remembered what I had said to him about savage taboos and being left alone with your mother-in-law; how if you got caught they sterilized you for good, chopped it off completely and gave it to Diana, decked in tinsel, maybe; and drove a spear through your unclean heart as well, and buried you deep, without so much as a bowl of gruel and no beads.

I could see Steve not standing up for his mother-in-law, but didn't she put a hex on him because he didn't? So he didn't respect, wasn't scared of her "mystery"! "What do you want more than anything in the world?" "Gussie." "Then kiss my foot." "Not me." "Then Gussie will sleep with the others."

And that's just what Augusta did.

Steve's almost violent ambivalent passion for his sweetheart's mother makes me wonder: Did he dream of her? I dare not ask. But it is clear that like a dragon she guarded the bedroom of the princess; like a horrid monster, a cold-breasted witch, she slept in the vestibule. What were her demands and what had the young men suffered who were allowed the drawing room? Had she felt them all over and asked them intimate, indecent questions? How much money have you got? What does your father do for a living? What was your mother's maiden name? Have you been circumcised? Are you a Jew? Perhaps she demanded their virginity in return for her daughter's maidenhead, I don't know. Did they, with the exception of Steve, stand up for mama and lie down with Augusta?

"Augusta is not at home, young man."

The Hookers were not new in town, but a little removed from it; geographically they lived in a comfortable, but déclassé, one might say, old house, colonial outside and mid-victorian inside, a mile out of the village; and in other ways Mrs. Hooker believed herself to be superior to, apart from, the village families. On the other hand she and her family were not noticed by the county people who live, as always, in a fringe outside of town with landscaped grounds, box hedges, horses and dogs, servants and credit. I do not think they knew she existed; were perfectly innocent of ill feeling or snobbery. Mrs. Hooker was the snob, and like a snob lived and breathed in a kind of unhappy vacuum, not caring to associate with people she thought were common and not accepted by those she secretly suspected of being her betters. How all this came about is too long a story, a kind of social erosion and interchange of state, perhaps, taking generations, and causing heartbreak and frustration, I've no doubt. Mrs. Hooker knew, for instance, that the old lady who lived in such style on the hill and whose daughters had married so well and whom the other gentry ingratiated, had been nothing more than a pretty parlor maid in the home of rich Mr. Aldrich whose first wife had been a Miss Johnson but frigid. She knew that the Turnbulls on Wayward Road who rode to the hounds and had bedded the then Prince of Wales had got rich in the grocery business, and that one of the girls had had an illegal operation and a niece was simple-minded. Some of this information came from the sewing woman who enjoyed the interest she evoked by telling tales from house to house, but most of it was almost legend, inherited. Mrs. Hooker herself was the daughter of a New England clergyman, whose father was also a clergyman, whose father was a doctor, and so was his, and she could prove it. That she was, nevertheless, a very vulgar woman may have been entirely her own fault. Mr. Hooker, Augusta's father, was a pleasant gentleman without any ambition whatever and quite content with his lot. His only interest was insects, which he collected and classified, and he had no interest at all in mammals. He did not care whether they lived in a house on the hill or in tanks; they more or less disgusted him by their very size, I think; he loved the wiry, the stem-like, the frangible. He could remove the proboscis from a male mosquito without hurting it and tend a seasick spider. But he was sweet and good to the big creatures with whom he was thrown by species and accepted Augusta, his only fertile seed, when she came, as politely as if she had been a dragonfly with iridescent wings. His preoccupation with the seemingly perverted sex relationships of insects: can-nibalism, trophallaxis, parabiosis, lestobiosis, polyandry, adelphogamy, adelphophagy, hermaphrodite(ism), was deep, and he would sit in his library, tense with excitement, wiping the mist that formed on his eyeglasses impatiently away as he read the big saga of sex among the very little folk. He sought in the woods and in the yard and on the pond for examples of entomological abandon among the wordless articulates, enlarged through his magnifying glass, and he kept a little notebook with two cryptic words written on it: *Examples of.* He loved to watch the frenzied seizures of flies in the sun. And he wore a black smock to attract them.

"Look, Gussie, watch!" he would say to the little girl.

"Denton!"

"But Fanny . . ."

"It's disgusting; you ought to be ashamed!"

Maybe it was and maybe he ought to be, but it was his only sex life and harmless enough. Once or twice a year he lectured at Harvard and Williams College but only once at Bryn Mawr in 1902. Mrs. Hooker approved of these scholarly connections or I think she would have drowned or swept out the lot of his almost progeny. "The orgasm of the dragonfly lasts astonishingly long," he wrote in his little book: Tuesday, July First. Timed a pair of dragonflies over Eustis Pond, one mile south of Gunning Point. Time: Seven minutes.

Gussie loved rowing him on the pond fed from fresh water springs surrounded by willows, and even enjoyed the bitter taste of rancid nuts he carried in his pocket for their "tea." While the professor, his jowls pink, a sweet dreamy look on his face, sat upright, haloed by gnats the color and density of gunpowder, a stop watch in hand, eyeing a pair of rainbow-shaped dragonflies, she watched the little turtles slip off the partly submerged tree trunks and waited, as patiently as her father did for the collective coitus among the minutiae, for an awkward turtle to climb up on her motionless oar by mistake.

"Look, daddy!" she whispered, "isn't he sweet?"

"Quiet! Wait, wait, Gussie; don't talk." He snapped his watch shut. "Now, child, what is it?"

"Oh daddy!" The snap of the watch had sent the little turtle back into the water. She saw him just under the surface hurry back to his friends on the stump to tell them about it. They stretched their necks out and up and Gussie saw their black lips shine as she let the boat slide silently past them.

That evening when they returned Mrs. Hooker said, "Old Harry Aldrich called you; what for? Remember, Denton, Sadie Aldrich has never taken the trouble to call on me, and you are not to go there."

Taking up the telephone, the professor began to tremble as he listened, "You don't say so! . . . You don't say so! . . . Is it possible! . . . You aren't sure? . . . It's a little far north for them but it could be. Don't do anything; I'll be right up."

Without waiting for an argument, Mr. Hooker got out of the house on the run, his baggy pants whipping against his legs as skinny as a mosquito's pasterns.

"Howdy do—down in the basement, Professor."

Mr. Hooker didn't have to look twice; without a word he placed his spatula-like thumb against the woodwork and it gave to his touch; he stripped off a narrow splinter of wood and surprised the preoccupied termites busy with their social antics.

"Gad!" said Harry Aldrich.

"Sweet Jesus!" said the professor raptly.

"Well," said Aldrich, "I understand if you cut off their water supply . . ."

Hooker turned on him.

"What!"

"They're eating the house up—or down—Gad, tell me what to do."

Hooker sat down, he felt weak, on the basement steps. "Aldrich," he said, "I've waited for this all my life."

Harry Aldrich looked embarrassed as if the professor were confiding in him about the laundress or wanted to borrow a ten-spot.

"Look here, old chap, I'll get you a drink. Watkins!"

"Aldrich, old man, let me stay here in your basement; live here. I must find the queen!"

"Ha! Ha! Ha!" exploded Aldrich, I don't know if he winked. "*Cherchez la femme,* eh?"

"Look, I'll go along with you," said Hooker eagerly, a clever look came into his pale blue eyes. "There are two ways to get rid of this particular species—two!" He held up two fingers.

"Get rid of 'um; I'll pay you well; oh, I beg pardon, Hooker, but I'll be grateful."

"Two ways. One you seem to know . . ."

"Encyclopedia Britannica, Eleventh Edition," said Aldrich apologetically.

"Well, that is cut off their water supply. Have you the plans of this house? No? I suspect the foundation is all wood; we'll have to pour concrete, cut them off from the ground. They'll die without water. Number two," said Hooker. "Find the queen, and," he shuddered, "destroy her." He waited, and said, "Without her they are lost, frantic; they will die, even with water at hand, they will not eat or drink; they will commit—like mass suicide."

"I say!" said old Aldrich, impressed. "You've got my permission to find the queen; go ahead, old chap. But will you recognize her? How?"

"She will not have the creamy white abdomen of a nymph," Hooker said as if talking to himself.

"Good lord no, old man!" said Aldrich.

"But I can't miss her; she will be twenty-four hundred times the volume of the workers and the soldiers, and she will be a pale strawberry yellow with reduced compound eyes."

"Look here, Hooker, how about a drink? I'll get it me'self," and he climbed up the stairs to tell his wife about the crazy fool in the basement. "Gad, he tickles me!"

"On the other hand," said Hooker shrewdly to himself, "if some *accident* happens to the real queen—if I should

take her away, perhaps—then I should witness her replacement; that is, in this particular species which I think
we have here, at this season, in this part of the country,
I should be the lucky man to witness a replacement! *If* this
is the macropterous type, and I think it is, a complemen-
tary female of the second or third form will replace the
first form original queen! She is a substitute queen. She
will have, I think, a creamy white belly, but I am not sure.
Dear God in Heaven, help me to fool Aldrich. This colony
must not be destroyed!"

Upstairs Mrs. Aldrich graciously received him and gave
him a cup of tea.

"Tomorrow," he said innocently to his host, "if you'll
get some workmen over we'll shut off the water supply."

"Thanks, old man, thanks no end."

"We are very grateful, Professor," said Mrs. Aldrich,
"I trust your wife is well?"

"Oh yes, ma'am, she's doin' as well as can be expected."
The professor felt full of fun. And he went home with
something damp and sightless in his pocket, with a pale
strawberry-colored abdomen; royalty.

That night Mr. Hooker stayed late in the library brush-
ing up on termites (he was ready and eager to masticate
wood for the queen, himself, and let her take it from his
tongue, if need be; he would tenderly groom her). But
being a professor, and generous, he wished to share his
experience and knowledge, and as Gussie was asleep he

tried to get Mrs. Hooker's attention. "Take trophallaxis, Fanny my dear, listen, 'Termites constantly groom or lick the surfaces of each other's bodies to obtain secretions or exudate which they eagerly solicit. The procedure is to stroke the body with the antennae, then groom the body with the mouth, or solicit directly from the mouth or anus of another termite. Many actions and reactions of termites may be explained by this eagerness for exudate or a desire for special forms of nourishment obtained by grooming, or solicited from another termite or colony guest. . . . Termites assiduously groom each other by licking. . . .' "

"Denton Hooker!"

"Yeah Fanny, my dear?"

"You're drunk! How dare you!"

"Come now, Fanny."

"It's positively indecent and immoral."

A quiet dignity came over Mr. Hooker and he said with great assurance, "We must not confuse morals with behavior." He was quoting Thomas Elliot Snyder, Senior Entomologist of the Bureau of Entomology and Plant Quarantine of the United States Department of Agriculture.

"It's still disgusting," said Mrs. Hooker soothed a little, it is true, by authority as quoted.

"Aren't you a trifle anthropocentric?" asked Mr. Hooker, edging toward the door.

"I'm what!"

"It just means a horse thinks everybody else is a horse,"
he said, and he snapped his fingers smartly on her rump
expecting her to buck and she did. "Ha!"

"I will not submit to your indignities!" she cried out.
"And what's more, don't you dare read that filthy book
to Augusta; I—I gave *birth* to her!" She was near tears.

"Yes," said her husband, quick to take advantage of her
weakness. "And you know what a termite or a bee would
think of that? A mighty nasty exhibition! Yes, ma'am."

Just then the casement window blew open and a great
bee trundled in, heavy with pollen. It looked like a nugget
of gold under the lamp.

"Ahh," said the professor.

"Shut the window!" screamed his wife.

He picked up the exhausted bee and left the room.
"Tired, dear?" he said to the little creature, "Heavy
laden?" Back in the library, "The old whore," he muttered. "If she were an *ant* they'd hang her up and *milk*
her! Good for her, too."

CHAPTER NINE

Well, that was Augusta's immediate ancestry; a queer miscegenation of viviparate and articulate. It is difficult to visualize the consummation of the mammal and the entomologist, and perhaps we shouldn't. Not being as curious as the professor, neither shall we time it. Nor shall we compare this likewise "fantastic marriage" further, to the point where, after copulation, "the lady flies away directly her seminal vesicles are sufficiently full of sperm . . . and the husband does as other ants (♂) do—he perishes."

But as Augusta grew up and was tutored at home by a triumvirate consisting of a ramshackle tramp of a schoolteacher, Fanny Hooker, and the professor (because she was a little too good for public school, it appeared), I think her homework included Forel on *Ants* and the *Social Register*, one being the social activity of insects, the other of mammals.

At puberty, because she was very pretty, Mrs. Hooker

broke into an ancestral piggy-bank and enrolled her in a girl's school, not too fashionable, but decent, a stone's throw, the glance of an eye, as it were, from the ———— Military Academy. I give Mrs. Hooker credit for the strictest economy at home during these years and it is the only credit she had. From a natural penury she subtracted even further thrift and they got along, as the saying goes, on a shoestring. It didn't bother the professor, who managed on as little as any of the hymenopterous creatures with whom he associated (he could have subsisted on distilled water from a disinfected sponge) and whose domesticity and evolution, or philogyny, absorbed him. His brain, ganglia, and nerves were keyed to theirs, and except for a gentler, almost noble expression, he resembled his minute friends; the dorsal and ventral aspect of the head were certainly similar. But Mrs. Hooker's disposition did not improve, and she was too proud to solicit anything at all.

Gussie came home from school the day Steve's father threw a wrench at him. The coincidence may have been in their stars, something interstellar, I do not know; Steve as you remember was born under the sixth sign of the zodiac, so simply for the astrological record, I find that Augusta's sign was the eleventh: Aquarius. She had not been home a week before young males seemed to spring up out of the ground like asparagus in early summer. In no time at all she seemed to know all the young men whose mamas hadn't taken the trouble to call on her mother. Gussie was exceptionally pretty with no affectations or quirks; not a tic disturbed the vivid serenity of her lovely face. I do not mean that the face of Augusta was expressionless or that it had but one expression. I mean that the many expressions that succeeded each other across it were unaffected and uninhibited; from gloom to joy, from tears to smiles, there was no conflict, no attempt to hide anything or pretend, so that the effect in the end was one of serenity. It was as much pleasure to watch Augusta's face as it is to observe a volatile summer sky. And many a young man stared at it as if it were a weather map indeed and his safety depended upon his knowing it by heart; and it was a dependable face, it didn't lie. If she had been one of her father's virgin nymphs with a creamy white abdomen she couldn't have attracted more suitors. And as often as Mother Hooker picked them off her, as it were, as sedulously did they return, as intent and single-minded, to destroy themselves, it would appear, as the little but lecherous beasties we've been talking about. Augusta, too, was as innocent as the innocent polyandry accepted by the female hymenoptera, and no unwholesome, as it is called, eroticism, disturbed her dreams or was reflected in her face. She had spent four years in a decent boarding school, a stone's throw, as I have said, from a young gentlemen's "military academy," and had picked up a little but not much. She had not been curious enough to become experienced. She was so pretty! (What

I am trying to say is: a very pretty woman does not need to go hunting and looking in corners to reassure herself; she is as fearless as a brave captain at sea. She knows that beauty is the best thing in the world and he knows that courage is, and neither will fail either if he's really got it.) The sudden quiet in a girl's dormitory when they can bear it no longer, the longing endured through seemingly endless days of geography, geometry, George Eliot and Henry James, chemistry and iambic pentameter, climaxed by involuntary and spontaneous, almost, relief, in the arms of like sufferers, she miraculously, one might say, escaped or missed. The evil, because they knew, elderly supervision of scrawny female intellectuals, anxious to get rid of innocence in their pupils because it was somehow on their minds and made them angry and frustrated, Augusta somehow also missed, as if she also had, like Steve, a guardian angel. But unlike Steve never found out that it worked. She hadn't been given any tools and so did not acquire a skill. As for the boys' school, a stone's throw away, she did learn there the pleasure of admiration and the habit-forming desire for male attention. But Augusta was as innocent when she met Steve of—what happens, is the only way I can say it—between the sexes, as if she were still merely hungry in her mother's womb, or naked and half asleep, caressed by the negligible pressure of fresh air.

I know you aren't going to believe me, but Steve did it so gently that no one knew it. He didn't and Gussie didn't!

"Even at three thousand R.P.M., which is quite a modest speed, the whole complicated cycle of operations, involving, as it does, two complete revolutions of the engine, takes place in one twenty-fifth part of a second, while the inlet stroke takes place in approximately one hundredth part of a second. During that brief interval the valve has to open, the cylinder to fill with gas, and then the valve has to close. As the heads of the valves are subject to the full force and heat of the explosion, and in addition, the exhaust valve is swept by flaming gas for half a revolution every second revolution, it is obvious that very exacting demands are made upon the valves and their attendant mechanism."

And so we have a mutual seduction perfectly timed, a lovely equation, an equinox that could not possibly have happened under any other circumstances whatever on any other Thursday at half past six. It was as if someone had led Mrs. Hooker through a series of her own little events and irritations and approximations to a given point situated, well, down town to Halley's Drug Store. A perfect "social anarchist-communist system" involved a certain group of ants at the same time to "choose" at last to conduct the nuptial flight, exactly one day before the rainy season, at exactly six thirty o'clock, and it was not chance that placed the professor in just the right spot that they would seem to choose him to light upon for their planned parenthood, which they did, enchanting him. And on the way home he will be later even than usual in arriving because whether he knows it or not he will amuse himself further, and contrarily, because he has had enough, by luring a couple of click-beetles from their nocturnal amours with a piece of burning wood.

Besides these circumstantial aids to love, each little lover had taken nineteen years of preparation, and prerequisite courses, as it were, in what only looked like accidental education of the mind and senses. There are those who will think it might have been prettier with benefit of clergy, but mightn't the rigid blessing and the airless church have just upset, or disturbed, the balance of the tender saga? It is only a suggestion. And just as an addendum, wasn't Steve sitting now under Libra, just west of him: the balance? Did that help? I don't think Mother Nature had a thing to do with it, any more than Jack Frost or Father Neptune; she is the eternal bungler and is interested only in copulation and production; her very language is unfit, it seems to me, to describe the union I have chosen to describe in the cleanest analogy I can think of. (You will also notice I have tactfully left them alone for a while.)

Augusta will always lean on these perfect moments in her memory; will always feel a nostalgia for that first of all firsts that she had not planned on. But Steve will forget for the same reason, which makes the difference in each of them rather than in what happened to each. Steve will forget because there was no distortion to keep it alive in his memory, no irritation to call his attention to it. Only the incompetent and the dissatisfied wear a hair shirt.

That I have led, in this manuscript, at least observed, Steve from birth through childhood and boyhood and adolescence only to place him in the arms of a little woman at half past six on Thursday may seem much-ado-about-nothing or a tour-de-force, and you will not believe the impression, at least, I have given, that the earth stood still while it happened and that every little thing and creature aided and abetted, and tactfully refrained from peeking at, the seduction that no one had planned but everyone had contributed his mite to. But do not forget that every hair on your head is numbered and every virginity accounted for and every one of us is made in the image of God, which entitles Steve to his niche, I think, and to his scribe. And as I am his scribe I must try to be as faithful as possible to the truth as it comes to me, and so I cannot be sure, as God is, about the loss, as it is quaintly called, of virginity; I cannot say. I was not there. No one was there; no one, no creature looked. It seems to me, then, that there are no witnesses and Steve and Augusta are as innocent as before it happened. There's got to be a witness to evil, for instance, to make it evil, and the witness has to be evil, too. Right? That the loss of virginity is, besides, an empty metaphor, I am convinced of. Steve no more lost his virginity at half past six than he lost his good looks. And as when something is lost the implication is that it will be found, when someone finds Augusta's there will be time, I think, enough to reconsider my suggestion, which is all it is, that neither is she minus anything at all.

I have given the lovers time, now, and I will return to them.

"I love you, Steve."

"I love you, Augusta," said Steve and added, "of course," as if it were hardly necessary to speak of it at all.

"I want you to marry me," he said. "Will you, Gussie?"

"Of course."

And it was "of course." Steve wasn't asking her to marry him from experience in ethics or out of what is called duty. He had not read any novels and Gussie hadn't paid attention to her mother's sporadic and irritable little lectures re: "How much is it?" and, "Always insist on a receipt." Steve certainly did not feel he had harmed her, or that he should give her an I.O.U.

In fact the first shock Steve got, and it should not have been much of a shock because it had become almost a refrain, was:

"Augusta is not at home, young man."

All Steve wanted was to be with Augusta forever and for always. At the moment that he had asked her, "Will you marry me?" he had not even felt desire and did not expect ever to feel it again. He had given everything he had to Augusta and he did not know that it was renewable. He did not, and he was right, compare this consummation with any of the sensual satisfactions of his past: the purely physical libidinous phenomena that purified temporarily his blood and his senses until the next time; the madness without subject matter. As for idolatry, the specific kind he had felt for John, that was over. This, as I have said, was an equation. He and his girl were equals, share and share alike. He had given her pleasure and so had she, him; and besides, a warmth and affection that was too new to be named, and too precious to lose. It must be and would be . . . forever, a kind of divine monogamy. The right bolt was in the right place; they were a double-synchronizing unit, maybe. And the Delta was there. Steve wasn't fickle, he hadn't forgotten the engine; he simply had stepped aside, avoiding the violence of the wrench, and found next door the same thing with something extra, less abstract than the machine.

It was as if each had been given a secret mixture: one part aphrodisiac and two parts sodium pentothal. As if Someone on High had said, "These are my children and this is their youth; gradually, and dram by dram, I will take away what I have given until they can endure life without it. The symptomatic pain of withdrawal may or may not be theirs."

Steve had been sent for, you see, to mend the boiler, and Gussie had gone down in the basement to show him where it was.

"This is the way," and it was.

Steve had followed her down the steps and his first look at Gussie had been from behind, lit up by his flashlight. It was as if he had never seen anything like it before and there was nothing to be afraid of. He saw the back of a glossy dark head, a slender neck with a mole on it, her shoulder blades moving under her blouse, a slim waist, and round buttocks that moved up and down rhythmically; the flat backs of her thighs, the hollow hinge of her knees, her rounded cálves; thin hard ankles and round heels that slipped in and out of kid slippers. Down below she had stayed with him; hovered near by as he worked, humming a little tune, "And Then My Heart Stood Still."

"Augusta!"

"Coming, Mother!"

Steve felt a kind of violence in that short dialogue but did not turn his head. He felt soft fingers on his neck, and smelled a sweet smell. He needed nothing more; turning on his haunches he took Augusta in his arms and searched in the semi-darkness for her mouth. When he had found it he did not hesitate to let go with one arm and search between her legs for something else, which was right there. It was as if he had kissed two mouths with one kiss. It had not lasted any longer than you could count ten. That was the meeting, the first meeting, and the beginning of a temporary separation between Steve and Gussie.

("Augusta is not at home, young man.")

For the first time Christina had said, really at a loss, "What is the matter, Steve?"

And for the first time Steve had said coldly, "Nothing," and added almost cruelly, "Why?" His first equivocation.

That "why" fell on Christina like the end of a mother's world, like some kind of frigid cancellation. How could she sit down and write a thesis on "Why?" It was better to give up and turn to Anna, who would some day say, "I don't know what you are talking about, Mother."

"Denton!"

"Ma'am?"

"I said will you speak to Augusta."

"Why sure I'll speak to her, 'course I will. Gussie!"

"No, you fool, not now!"

"When?"

"I told you, at just the right time."

"When will that be, Fanny, because I've got to be going."

"You will have to figure it out yourself."

"O.K., that's what I'll do."

"Do you remember what I told you to say?"

"Oh yes, well, I'm off."

"Augusta, did your father speak to you?"

"What, Mother?"

"Did—your—father—speak—to—you?"

"But, Mother, I don't understand; of course Daddy always does."

"Did he speak, I mean, about that boy?"

"What boy?"

"Augusta!"

"Yes, Mother."

"You cannot deceive me; I am not as simple-minded as your father."

"I think Daddy is very complex."

"We are not talking about your father."

"But . . ."

"Don't contradict me, Augusta!"

The young gentlemen from near-by estates and country houses began to fall away, and Gussie did not seem to notice or care. All of them had kissed her on the mouth; all of them had held hands with her; one or two had fondled her a little and hoped for more the next time. Gussie was tractable, docile, compliant, without any plans. She did not find the young men repulsive, neither did they awaken desire in her any more than the boys a stone's throw away at the ———— Military Academy had. She was like a lovely collie. And I am afraid the young gentlemen in the neighborhood resembled in their behavior the village mongrels who couldn't really help it. They were a good-looking lot (the boys) and Gussie absorbed a heap of Vitamin D from the sunshine of their undisguised admiration. It prepared her quite adequately for Steve. When she had preceded him to the cellar that evening she was expecting young Dawson, the one with blue eyes and dark lashes and long legs, in an hour, but she saw no harm, did not even consider the idea of harm, in placing her hands on Steve's neck, a little under his collar, because at the moment she did it she wanted to. I think Gussie always made the normal feminine first advance that all normal femininity makes. Sometimes it is that first look, unrestrained, as if you pulled up the shade in your eyes, sometimes a touch that really means it, sometimes an almost succulent caress in the voice, but it is always recognized. If a girl like Gussie didn't do it just as she always did, modestly and sweetly but earnestly, the boys like the boys I am talking about would never have the courage, perhaps, nor the inclination, certainly not the initiative, to make the first advance themselves. It's like waiting for the spark before you add the kindling. She enkindled them like a lot of twigs, too. Forked ones. But Augusta didn't invite rape. No one, drunk or sober, would ever force himself on her. She wasn't like that. And of course I don't have to say that Gussie was no snob. She didn't spring from her mother's brow, wasn't nourished on her notions, and inherited none of her acquired characteristics. Steve was good-looking and the round neck enticing; it was immediately time for the first caress and so she did it; and Steve, you remember, who had seen nothing but her back, which was wonderful, responded. For a few moments he held the passive Gussie close and caressed her in the right places. If Gussie had been used to thinking, she would have thought, "Here is something new under the sun."

A certain repressed and easy confident violence in Steve's embrace excited her—and here we are back at the dialogue.

"Augusta!"

"Coming, Mother."

And Steve had sensed violence in it. Augusta! It did cross his mind—but slipped away. I mean the conditioned response of his body, which is a good thing; it's a good thing it did slip away.

He finished his job, able as he was to step over into another alley, as it were, and concentrated on whatever it was; percussion maybe. He left the house quietly and that is when, upon his arrival, his mother had thought, "What is the matter, Steve?" and had asked him out loud. "Nothing," he had replied. "Why?"

Mrs. Hooker said a queer thing, at least it seems queer if you don't know how a motivated mother can cover a lot of ground and a lot of subjunctives in a short time in her mind as regards her daughter's future, when Gussie came back upstairs.

"His mother, I understand, is the granddaughter of _____ __________ ___________________, the first Bishop of the State." She meant, I suppose, to say it to herself. Her pride was grasping at a straw, a kind of, in this case, reed, with religious significance. True he had come to mend the boiler but he could not be riff-raff, common, if his great-grandfather had mended, in good taste and impeccably dressed, souls; souls, no doubt, of the owners of yachts, dressed in flannels and haloed in yachting caps. This is not as arbitrary and imaginative or mixed a description as it might appear, on my part. Odds and ends of the insignia of the privileged did float about in poor Mrs. Hooker's head. Her subconscious was crammed with puny and tinkling symbols of position and inheritance and influence. In her dreams she anxiously studied menus *à la français*, wondering what she should order. It wasn't easy.

"I don't know," said Gussie. "Really? You mean a *minister?*" and a thin pain slid down the insides of her thighs as she recalled Steve's hands caressing her there. Teddy Dawson—who had been rather spoiled by Gussie because his black lashes were so pleasantly startling, surrounding his sky-blue eyes, which had led her, as her first advance, to run her forefinger over them and say, "Nice"—didn't stay long. Gussie was as beautiful as ever, but it was as if a sliding door had closed; her eyes were as dark and glowing but without a deep place to go into; impervious. Her hands were soft and smooth and warm but did not cling or linger. When he kissed her and said, "Gussie," just as he had planned, nothing that he had planned happened. In his daydream she had returned his embrace passionately and he had said, "I love you passionately, you are the only woman for me," and she had said, "I love you, too, passionately," and had succumbed almost immediately on the sofa with garlands on it to his terrible desire. Passion! He had not known how to undress her or really how to do it but it had come about and they were lovers and the other fellows all knew. None of it happened; the sequence didn't develop. Gussie was polite and sweet and even affectionate because that is what she was like, but Steve had put an end, for the time being, anyway, to her funny female philandering, and she wanted Teddy to go away. He did; that's how easy it was, and no tragedy, no matter how you look at it.

Mrs. Hooker noted from her casement window, as it were, the retreating forms of eligible and desirable young men, the sons of, the sons of, the sons of, and with decent incomes, too, and nice manners; respectful boys who stood up when she came in the room.

Then the ramshackle tramp of a tutor, who wore a signet ring with a pale false ruby on his little finger and moistened his dry lips with a bluish tongue before he came out with the atrocity, waited on the mother of the beautiful and sensuous Augusta and dared, in his impudence, in his too tight and fitted-at-the-waist jacket and his shiny pants and pointed shoes, to ask for her only daughter's hand. Hand! Mrs. Hooker's gentility did not save her from a crass and vulgar, nasty vision. Hand! Christ! In stifling the vicious picture in her mind, followed by the insulting vignette of his accompanying them to Trinity Church on Sundays, Mrs. Hooker's whole immense body shook with the struggle to remain a lady and keep from spitting on the poor and scrawny fool. But again she became articulate

with unexpectedly collected words, "I will call Augusta";
she simpered and almost winked; she had turned a bilious
yellow.

"Augusta!"

"Yes, Mother. . . . Oh hello, Stinky!"

"Augusta, Mr. Gentian has asked for your hand."

"Put it there, Stinky," said Augusta, holding out her
hand and laughing. "Oh I'd love it, only I don't want to
get married; not for a long time. Let's play Canasta and
then I have to go to the movies; I promised. Is that O.K.?
Stinky?"

No one knows where Augusta's sweet poise came from;
or else she felt nothing at all. She didn't see anything lu-
dicrous, it appeared, in the poor fellow's temerity; she
wasn't the least insulted; she did not even seem to recognize that her mother was near collapse; and Mrs. Hooker's
spontaneous strategy, her bead-like mind's thought that
this sudden introduction to Augusta of the depths she
might face, that it might bring her to her senses, failed
completely. I like Augusta; she had, what you might call,
a quiddity, an ego, something cardinal and inherent, indigenous. But I don't know where it came from. It probably took as many eons as moss to learn to grow on the
north side of an oak did; tact.

"Rock of ages cleft for me," sang Augusta in a throaty
tender voice as she went off to meet Steve at Eustis Pond.

CHAPTER TEN

And then, as you know, it was bound to become six-thirty on that Thursday I told you about. The day marked by the preordained nuptial flight of the hymenoptera; the interrupted amours of click-beetles; Mrs. Hooker's nicely timed trip to Halley's Drug Store for some pills for her recurring bilious attacks; and the assumption of the *toga virilis* by Steve.

Augusta, the nubile maiden, became really marriageable. All on Thursday at half past six.

But no date was set for the wedding; not because it would never take place, and it didn't, but for no particular reason at all. Augusta had said, "Of course," and meant it, but liked things the way they were, the sweet *status quo;* she even used the same words to her beloved Steve as to the-ramshackle-one, "Not for a long time."

"But, Gussie, I want to soon," said Steve.

"Only not now."

"No, not right now, but soon."

"Oh yes soon, naturally."

Gussie agreed with Steve because she was compliant, but she seemed to want not to plan and a wedding meant planning. She wasn't afraid of her mother, discounted her malevolence and her ability; Gussie never quarreled with anyone and so she never felt she was being thwarted and I don't suppose she was. Mrs. Hooker wasted a lot of energy delivering her philippics which had no more effect than if she were delivering The Sermon on the Mount to the freshman class and Gussie didn't seem to have a receiving set, she wasn't grounded. You couldn't make a scene with Gussie either. She would seem to disappear, not entirely, but almost, like the cat in *Alice in Wonderland.* But she did exist, she did endure; she was a little woman of feeling, not so much feeling as feelings. I would say she thought with her blood but it seems too violent a metaphor. Let us say she went along with her antennae.

But Steve, more fastidious, felt the pressure against him in "the next room." When he held Gussie in his arms and enjoyed her and himself, loved her with all his being, everything was all right. She cast a spell over him. If she had asked him to kiss her mother's foot at that moment he would have. But in between times the male in him that had been spellbound inside his sweetheart was frustrated and, interrupted, you might say, by that hostile female in the "next room" who ought to be raped. The words, "sack, pilfer, filch, prig, bag, crib, crimp, fleece, diddle, mulct, rook, bilk, pluck, rustle, poach," came to his mind in

time with the beat of his heart. How he longed to despoil
her! This is really what he said to himself. He hated her
and wished to rape her. The old lady represented confusion, noise, violence, fear, the loss of free-will, almost of
manhood, castration really, and he had but one weapon,
one expression, and he knew how it worked. Don't leave
him alone with her! It is punishable by death! It is incest!

Well.

"Gussie?"

"Steve, darling?"

"Don't you know your mother hates me?"

"Oh no, Steve."

"She won't let you marry me."

"We'll be married some day; mother just likes to fuss."

"Fuss? She'd prune me!"

"Funny Stevie."

"What has she against me?"

"She says you don't stand up when she comes in the
room."

"No I don't," said Steve, adding to himself, "And that
I never will!"

"But why don't you, Steve, it wouldn't hurt you, would
it?"

"Yes, it would." Steve couldn't explain the symbolism
of standing up for a bitch and what it would do to
him, probably not even to himself. And as it wasn't likely
that the bitch would be present while he was spellbound,

and as it would not enter Augusta's head to ask him favors in the midst of their nuptial flights, he never would get to his feet, that I believe.

Time passed for everyone but the little lovers; the spring and the summer and the fall and the winter were hardly noticed. Augusta lived with Steve actually and in her dreams; nothing else could touch her. But as Steve's love for his girl increased, so did his curious hatred for her mother. Then one afternoon Mrs. Hooker caught them. She really had not meant to spy; she knew enough, too much, without hunting for evidence. It was a warm August day, and Denton was rowing himself alone on Eustis Pond, surrounded by three sets of dragonflies at equi-distance . . . dragonflies have a peculiar sense of the distance of safety . . . from the boat, and he was as thrilled as a child at a three-ring circus. A call had come from the Associated Press re an article Denton had had published in the *Insect World*, and Mrs. Hooker went to find her husband. The reporter had intimated that the magazine was to be "taken off the stands," whatever that meant. Denton, I suppose, had polished up a copulation scene a little too enthusiastically. Mrs. Hooker saw Steve lying on his back in the shade and Augusta taking the initiative. She was on her hands and knees straddling him like a little vixen over her young; her round breasts hung down; and Steve lay quiescent, his head to one side, his eyes closed; only his hands caressed the nymph between her legs. As Mrs. Hooker watched, speechless and horrified but terribly attracted, the girl suddenly dipped her head and bit Steve in the neck. As she lost her "four-legged" stance, she rolled to Steve's side and they began to play and laugh. You wouldn't have known whose legs were whose except for Augusta's shorts and Steve's faded jeans; they were bare-footed; Steve wore no shirt and Augusta's blouse lay folded neatly under a bush. Mrs. Hooker turned and skirted them. She was the evil witness; the *corpus* and the *delicti* had been found. It was time for the cross-examination.

That night Steve rang the doorbell as usual. The answer he expected was, "Augusta is not at home, young man," and as usual he expected to see Gussie trot down the stairs calling out, "Come on in, Steve," and Mrs. Hooker would step aside, unequal to the occasion. But Mrs. Hooker said instead, "Come in young man, Augusta . . ." I don't know what she said about the whereabouts of Augusta.

That was the night Steve lost his virginity.

"I saw you," said Mrs. Hooker, "and you are a dirty boy!"

"Saw me?" said Steve. "How?"

"How indeed! Right in the path to Eustis Pond! I could have stepped on you!"

It was true it had come over them in the middle of a languid stroll and they had not bothered to do more than step aside and lie down under a tree.

To Steve it was as if someone had uncovered him as a little boy, awakening from one of his divine dreams, which you remember he had been spared. Shame mixed with anger came over him in a great fluent wave and left him trembling and sore all over. The blush throbbed in his throat.

"I see you have the decency to blush."

Steve had never blushed before, had never felt the need to, and he waited for it to go away before he spoke.

"I quit," he said.

He had not known what vernacular he would use, or even exactly what he meant. He left the house without having seen Augusta and went to a movie in the village.

It didn't happen as fast as I have written it and I didn't expect Steve to "quit" like that so suddenly, but the time came and he did, as of course I knew he would, eventually; but his timing is better than mine. It had to happen just as, and when, he did it.

There had been conversations between the mother and daughter that didn't differ much from the conversations I have given you. In the back room of her mind Mrs. Hooker tried, because it looked as if she might have to, to accept Steve. She fondled visions of the Bishop received by the best people, and felt that it could, without too much ostentation, be introduced into the formal announcement in *The Chronicle* and be copied in the City papers as well. It also would get about, there was the sewing woman, and Denton might be persuaded to drop it, *sotto voce*, at the Aldrich's. But it was Augusta, herself, not in the least impressed with lineage, who said, "I wonder if the Portuguese sailor was good looking."

"What, Augusta, is a Portuguese sailor?" I think Mrs. Hooker really thought it might be a spring hat or a new middy.

"Steve's other grandfather was a romantic Portuguese sailor, he says."

"Ahh!"

"He fell in love with a Maine school teacher but they didn't have time to get married."

"Tell me more," said Mrs. Hooker sarcastically.

"He was a great lover."

"Indeed!"

"Yes, I think it's cute; he met the little school teacher at a dance in the parish house, and she fell madly in love with him. He took her to his boarding house down on the waterfront so he could watch for the tide and he didn't want to wake her up so early to say good-by. At five-thirty he left her. And I guess he must have drowned or something because he never came back. I think that is romantic and sad."

"It's indecent, Augusta, and you know it."

But Augusta didn't have the least idea.

"Steve has a wonderful new job, Mother."

"Yes?" Mrs. Hooker said faintly; even so late, there was a tiny piddling hope.

"He's driving a big Mack truck."

Something broke to pieces behind Mrs. Hooker's eyes like splintering glass; she felt a big black hole and a

draught where her mind used to be; it was as if she were
taking a terrible beating. What had her ridiculous and
hopeful tenacity suggested to her—that he might have
accepted the presidency of the Stock Exchange! She said
in a squeaky voice like the final whine of a deflated, child's
balloon, "That boy! That boy is a thief!"

"No, Mother, he didn't *steal* the truck and he makes
twenty dollars a week."

"He is positively immoral and he . . . he degrades me!"

"You? Steve?"

"Yes me. That boy."

If only Steve had known! It might have rid him of poison that he would have to get rid of elsewhere.

A week passed and Gussie was bored. Teddy called and
asked her to a dance at the Country Club. She was feeling,
for her, a little depressed.

"That's what you get for wearing your heart upon your
sleeve for daws to pick it," her mother had said. With a
little more energy, a little more desire, she would have
gone in search of Steve but she didn't quite make it. It
wasn't pride; she just wasn't up to it. She went to the
dance because it was simpler and met a young Frenchman
with a title of some sort, nothing much, a house-guest of
someone, and during supper at one-thirty, out in the pavil-
lion, she had let him do it. "You American virgins," he
had said, "you are so pretty and so cold; *insensible;* brrr."

They were dancing to a battered old victrola. Gussie
laughed. "Are you really a prince?" she said. She put one
hand under his jacket and felt around for a shirt stud that
she neatly snapped out; she slipped her whole hand to the
wrist inside his shirt and laid it against his skin. He
thought he was dreaming; he couldn't believe his senses,
not even his ears although they had turned pink; nor his
heart that changed its rhythm to a loud booming that
Gussie could easily hear, and she believed her ears, if he
didn't. He was slow, that's all. What a funny unfeminine
maneuver! *Quelle femme c'etait que!* But it only took a
second or two for the French schoolboy to translate it into
his mother tongue and not as gently as Steve, a little viciously, he responded *s'il vous plait.* The dance was scarcely
interrupted; the same waltz was playing when they finished
as when they began.

"*Merci!*" he whispered in her ear.

"*Il n'y a pas de quoi,*" she said, which means, "You're
welcome," but translated literally says, "It's not even of
what," or "It's less than nothing." Could she be right? But
I think this time it counted Up On High. It was put down
in one of God's Ledgers, the blue and scarlet one, marked
Sacred and Profane Love, with a line down the center.
Gussie was in the red. These two were their own witnesses.
I'm not excusing Gussie this time on the theory that it was
hardly of a whatness, debatable as that is, or that she
didn't know it was loaded. Nor Robert, because he didn't
understand English, and the whole thing, anyway, was ex-

temporaneous; *extempore;* without premeditation. And besides, God didn't go to the Harvard Law School. His is the Great Intuition and it is not as arbitrary as it may sometimes seem to us, the *habeas corpus.*

I hate to leave Gussie like this but Steve did; and she had meant almost beatitude to him as Beatrice had to Dante, only Beatrice had been Ginger's age and never really grew up. And there hadn't been at any of the symbolic levels a Mrs. Hooker to contend with. To date I know no more of what happened to Gussie than what Steve has said, "She married a working man after all and had five children." It would be foolish to try and extract a moral from this connubial eventuality or picture Gussie as losing her looks, her figure, her disposition, and her prestige, struggling over a rusty washtub with dirty children at her heels and a drunken husband asleep over the kitchen table, a big hound dog outside sniffing at an overturned garbage pail, the terrain and atmosphere suggesting the wages of sin. Gussie, it is true, had become rapidly promiscuous after Steve left her but Gussie just liked to please and didn't think what she had was priceless. The tall and handsome linesman, who spent three hours on the wires outside Gussie's window after the storm that did considerable damage in————County, spent an hour more on company time in Gussie's room, and after that had often taken the same short cut up the pole to reach the pretty and cheerful girl whom he soon grew to love with a gentle adoration. Gussie smoothed away the indentation of his

spurs on the chintz-covered bed. Mrs. Hooker hadn't had
time to consider his ancestry before his progeny were on
the way, and the night Gussie rode down the pole with her
legs around her sweetheart's waist and nothing but her
manicure set and two dollars, Mrs. Hooker scarcely stirred
in her sleep. And before she could reach Gussie's room
next morning to tell her that she was wanted on the telephone, Gussie was decently married and her tall husband
gone back to work. I wouldn't be surprised if Gussie made
a good wife, a pleasure to come home to, satisfied by the
everlasting admiration and attention of a tireless and
handsome beau. That he dug his spurs into wood rather
than into the heaving sides of polo ponies was of no conse-
quence to her, and if she had been romantic, his climbing
on high and talking to Sacramento and Albuquerque
might have tickled her imagination. But Gussie was a real-
ist, without inhibitions, without compulsions, perfectly
normal; and I must leave her now for that very reason.

Steve went to a movie, you remember. I think he went
there because it was dark, a place where he could not see
his hands, or sense the outlines of his body; where one's
friends and acquaintances and his brothers were incognito,
merely weights and measures obeying the laws and regula-
tions of Newton and Galileo; their minds in their pockets,
as it were, their lungs metabolic references only, their
hearts for cardiographic charts. With the ceiling zero, the

visibility zero, the dense and airless theatre was like a big
womb; the numberless fetuses elbow to elbow, knee to
knee; girls and boys in frightening embraces seeking each
other's mouths and genitalia. And on the bright silver
screen, violence: Unfinished sentences and unsolved mur-
ders, death without reason, ships keeling over, direst pov-
erty and absurd riches, anguished sobs; unbridled and illi-
cit passions and crazy cats; screaming ducklings; insane
laughter and bawdy jokes; altogether the terrible exag-
geration of life reduced to, but heightened by, the brightly
lit screen; all else in elemental darkness. And to this nos-
talgic madness these theatregoers will return again and
again, as if in remorse. It is home.

But Steve went there not so much to get back ("He
don't want to go back") but to get away. Perhaps without
knowing it he sought his guardian angel. But oblivion and
sweetness did not come to him this time after tragedy.
Evil was in his mind; he had been expelled from innocence; the sheet that had covered his limbs had been
raised by an evil witness and a cruel bluish daylight had
exposed his secret. To a bitch! How he longed, how im-
potently he longed, to straddle her, to milk her with his
teeth, tear open her thighs and split her in two with his
passion. How he wished to see the red hot blood spit out
of her like a geyser out of glistening rock. But with his
anger came impotence. Much as Mrs. Hooker deserved
this highly imaginative and therapeutic treatment, she
was safe.

Unable to sit through the interminable revelry on the

screen, the throb of the organ beating on his every membrane, the smell of human bodies sickening him, he stumbled over the knees and ankles of a row of unrecognizable and faceless neighbors and reached the aisle. Standing in the shadows at the back of the theatre was the dark still form of a girl and she caught at his sleeve. "Stevie!" she whispered, so close to his cheek that he smelled her sweet breath like vanilla. All the boys knew and talked of Evie. But he felt no temptation, no curiosity; nothing, not even the desire for comfort, or feminine cajolery.

"Let me go," he said. "No!"

"Sshh!" she warned him. "Stevie, please!"

"No," he said, feeling a softness come over him at the pathetic tone of her voice. "No," he repeated, firmly, "not me." And as the lights came on behind him, in the momentary stillness, after the organ and before the resumption of voices, he left the place and went home, knowing what he would do.

He changed from his good suit into his working clothes and on the way out he saw Anna standing by the window in one of her stillnesses, one of her daydreams. He hoped to get out without her noticing him, but she turned and saw him and smiled. "Brother Steve," she said almost inaudibly. Steve had a curious sensation as if he had been away for a long time, as he looked at the new strange girl, so cool, her eyes level with his. Anna was grown up! What a funny thing to have happen to him at such a time, such a split second between decision and action. He looked at her as if she were a picture on a calendar; he saw her curving brows, short nose, even her nostrils, her soft mouth. Then he sensed rather than saw her breasts; breasts on Anna! In the side light of the window one tip was outlined inside her almost transparent blouse, no bigger than a pink thumbtack. His thoughts traced her body downwards, the soft intake of her waist, the rest of her, the place between her slightly straddled thighs. He remembered her sensuous, preoccupied look when she was little (wasn't it yesterday!), when she stood before them all, her eyes round and unseeing, her hand high up between her legs. "Anna," Christina would say, "get me my needle and thread," and Anna would come to. "What, Mama?" Could this new and lovely creature be that same freakish little Anna? He felt a contraction in his insides, a strong and contrary desire for this girl, his sister. It was the instant between good and evil, sacred and profane love, and he not so much chose, since he was beyond choice, as he accepted, the latter. But not now, not Anna, the little stranger; she, too, was safe. As she turned back to the window, Steve noticed a green bruise over one temple. Sam, furious at a drawer that wouldn't open had shied an ashtray at her, called her for some reason, "A goddamn mouse."

"Anna . . ."

"Brother?"

But whatever he was going to say, perhaps nothing at all, no one remembers. He left that night in the big truck for Chicago.

CHAPTER ELEVEN

Every author at this point, every male author, at least, helps the boy with whom he has identified himself over a certain threshold into the next room. In almost every male memoir there is that next room: the brothel. Descriptions vary, experiences vary, but in every one the boy places his money in the till and is indebted to no one. He has honestly bought himself something, and goes out a free man, the beginning of irrelation. That in these memoirs he has sometimes, quite often, filched the cost from his mama does not seem to detract from the feeling of freedom. Indeed these special ones come out as cleansed, it would appear, if not more thoroughly so, than the other more normal ones. "How much?" *"Combien?" "Cuanto?" "Wie viel?"* And the dollars-and-cents, the francs, the pesetas, the reichmarks, the kronen, the guilders, the rupees, the liras, the yen, drachmas and, in Ecuador pleasantly enough, the sucre, sugar for sugar, are exchanged for a woman's body; not so much a woman as the woman. Symbolically, the boy, like Caesar who dreamed that he lay with his mother, has conquered the Earth; has rid himself of the strangling tentacles of devotion; divorced himself from his roots, the ambivalent and intolerable, incestuous love of his mother, his sister, his fiancée, his cousin, his governess, later on his wife; good women. That is what I mean when I say that the boy who steals the pennies from his mother's bureau drawer to pay for his pleasure is the special one who in this way doubles his enjoyment; the forbidden one who will not allow him to sleep with her has provided him with the means to straddle another in her image, and although he has paid for a woman another woman has treated him to her. These are the shenanigans of the hypersensitive and the perverse, but these are the ones who give us their memoirs. These are the ones who will to us their everlasting poetry—the flowers of evil, *Les Fleurs du Mal*; and ask us to spend, as they have, "A Season in Hell." And in between the lines we are bequeathed their hatred for mama; because they owe her forty francs, is that it?

None of this digression has much, if anything at all, to do with Steve. Steve is not a poet, close to the scaffolding of poets as is his, it may appear, erection. The possibility that he might have been (a poet), given as he was the poisoned pabulum, as it were, for his nourishment, about which I have tried to write—a big dose of Mrs. Hooker— I will leave to the next biographer, as I suspect another will take up where I leave off; I am not the last woman

in Steve's life. But there was, and is, something poetic
about Steve's love of the machine (couldn't he have written, "Her thighs are pistons, her womb is a tank and her
lust is velocity"?); his interest in the innocent orgasm of
lilies, his remark at just the right time, to give it analogi-
cal meaning, "There's a fungus on the rye."

There is something of the saint, too, in Steve, I think,
although I cannot prove it; the evidence has not yet become apparent. But the pattern is surely there, spreading
along the ground like the shadow of a big cross. But overhead, too many million light years away to cast any
shadow on our planet at all, the constellation of Libra, the
Balance, glows especially bright tonight as Steve, in the
cab of the big truck, heads, in a way, toward it; for it sits
just west of him, west of Virgo. Minutely then, he is
headed in the right direction, captious as his travels may
seem to the rest of us, and inglorious his compulsion. Like
St. Augustine, he *must* arrive at Carthage, and then, and
like the saint, indulge, as of a necessary and purifying ritual, in excesses and dissipation. "To Carthage then!"
(Book III) He might have chalked on the side of his
truck, "Carthage or Bust," and routes 13 and 6 will take
him there all right. Chicago lies ahead haloed in smog.

Steve began tidying up the guided missile, we might call
it, in which he was traveling. He did not need to think of
the truck or its mechanisms, it was in perfect order, and
he drove it by now as easily as he walked, without mental
or physical effort. His map lay beside him but he scarcely

needed to consult it. The route numbers repeated themselves, showing up in the glare of his headlights, slipping over the top of the truck, it seemed; disappearing in his mirror faintly pink from the bloody glow of his tail light. Steve shoved a dirty fluff of waste in the glove compartment. emptied a stinking ashtray out the window, destroyed an ancient map. He felt along the backs of the cushions and brought up two bobby pins and a dime. He began, in his loneliness, to think about the last driver of the truck. Off the floor he picked a yellowed carton smelling faintly of coffee, and a telephone slug. Back in the glove compartment again he found a match cover from a tavern in Calumet City and some colored toothpicks. He noticed that a lot of the cigarette butts had been brightly tinged with lipstick. He had cleaned up the cab pretty thoroughly when he thought of the light shades overhead. He reached up and pulled one down. Cards loosely clipped on slid off onto the seat. They were harmless enough: Girls on the beach with pointed bosoms and round buttocks and innocent, vacuous smiles, skimpy bras and three-cornered panties, polka-dotted and striped following the curves into recesses. Their skin was like freshly laid calcimine, slippery and cold, but they had, evidently, satisfied the truckdriver before Steve who had also had, judging by the pink cigarette butts, the bobby pins, realer company than that. Steve pulled down the other eye-shade and felt back into it; something soft seemed to respond to his touch and cling to his fingers. He drew out a little bunch of material, and the cab smelled of woman. A sweetness of talcum and femininity and lust surrounded him in the middle of nowhere as if he were a sparrow caught in a handkerchief. As he spread out his hand the thing, the perfumed bit of apparel, spread itself out like an apple blossom opening and the panties lay on his palm exactly as if he had just taken them off the girl himself. He sensed the negligible weight of her indenting the leather cushion beside him within easy reach of his hands; he felt the humidity of her breath and imagined that it formed round spots, condensing on his windshield. He slid down the window and in the draft of it something fluttered down onto his thigh: a snapshot. Just an ordinary girl in slacks and sweater, holding a puppy. On the other side it said, "I love you and so does Caesar." Then it said, "My mouth," and the girl had pressed her lips to the paper leaving a smeared red mark like two bows back to back. But someone had enhanced the imprint with a heavy lead pencil: Between the lips the tip of a tongue showed and if you held the card so that the mouth was vertical rather than horizontal, the effect was secret and devastating, as if the girl had sent him a passionate invitation indeed.

Steve stared at the scarlet symbol, disassociating it from the "blind date" and the puppy on the other side. Searching in his pocket, he took out a stubby pencil and licked it. He could not, it seemed, have done otherwise; with trembling fingers and the concentration of a schoolboy drawing a map of Florida he completed the drawing. It only took four curved lines, one each for the upper and lower profile of each thigh, one vicious period that broke the lead of his pencil to mark the navel, and all womanhood lay helplessly and pathetically exposed. Steve did it, because he could not help it, but it was an empty satisfaction, a cruelly impotent and abstract pastime; his body did not respond and anger built up in him. He tore the caricature of woman to bits until it lay like confetti under his heel, drifting into the clutch and the brake, sticking to the accelerator, sliding into the cuff of his trouser leg. And so "the dirty boy" drove on in the night toward Carthage.

Near morning he dozed, slowed up by a long line of trucks, loaded with vegetables, packed with chickens, bedsteads, spuds; the necessities; and his colleagues, separated only by the length of a truck, one behind him, one ahead of him, seemed to guide him, part as he was of an industrious fraternal migration, and not alone even in his dreams. (And don't you others, sublimating your libidinous impulses at the Stork Club, chomping on a T-bone, plunging pink shrimps into blood-colored sauce and smacking your lips as if you were devouring the ears of the chorus, be too quick to judge. A small closed room like the cab of a truck does not necessarily suggest claustrophobia, and temptation takes as many shapes as man in his ingenuity can imagine and she has not always shining teeth nor alabaster bosom. Perhaps a man alone at night, shut up in space, is reminded of those precious moments when as a little boy he is alone at last, his parents asleep,

and he is free to explore forbidden acres, anticipate the big
secret just around the corner.)

Steve drew up with the others at a dingy place marked
by a swinging sign that the sun shone on, attracting my-
riads of flies like extra periods, TRUCK DRIVERS WEL-
COME, and had his coffee; and like the others, he doused
his pair of flat fried eggs with bright red catsup that he
hammered out of a glass bottle with his palm as it passed
him. There was no conversation at this early hour; the
last man down saying only, "Jesus Christ," in a soft voice
when the catsup bottle went dry.

The touching beauty, so varied and full of surprises, of
New England in the fall lay far behind him; no cock-
pheasants ran along the side of the road, nor did their
hens, pretending they didn't see the big truck, deliberately
cross in front of him followed by their fat young ones. No
tall cats sat in the tawny fields waiting for field mice and
no smear on the asphalt suggested a careless furry
squirrel; he had looked in vain for yellow and red sugar
maples that John had taught him to recognize. The grayish land lay flat and interminable along either side of the
highway, like a huge and spongy fungus; battered signs
advertising the needs and luxuries of men, from wheaties
to hundred-proof bourbon, from burlesque to repentence,
seemed to float in the colorless sky over sterile land. There
seemed to be no horizon. Then he saw a pretty sight, and
he slowed down and crept by it to make it last longer. It
reminded him of nothing else; it was brand new; a post-

card from some extraneous place. In a sudden spotlighted apple orchard, like a painting hung on a wall, nuns were standing on stepladders picking big red apples. The wind tossed their wide flaring coronets like the whipping of balloon jibs on a dozen little sloops in a squall, swinging their great dun-colored skirts about their ample hips and tugging at their bosoms. But there was a stillness as of pantomime about the picture; the flat trunks of the trees seemed cut out of pasteboard; the gray background looked like house paint slapped on with an enormous brush. Nuns leaned over freshly shellacked baskets of crimson apples and nuns reached up into pale green foliage and passed the round fruit down to nuns below who raised their arms like caryatids to the smoky sky. Suddenly one of them, as spry as a deer, came racing after an apple that had spilled over and was rolling down an incline to the highway in front of him. It was as if she had broken out of the frame of the picture to play for a moment. She held out her hands and her mouth was open, her teeth shining. As she reached down for the apple Steve saw her breasts move inside her guimpe. He stopped his truck and leaned out; she was close enough to touch. She stood up and he could see her breathe; her cheeks were as red as the apples and her eyes bright and transparent as clear water.

"Hi!" said Steve.

The nun looked straight into his eyes and lifting her hand placed one finger on her lips. The others were all beckoning and watching in a secondary kind of silence and

Steve blushed. The nun just perceptibly shook her head,
smiled at him, and went back, much more sedately than
she had bounded out after the apple. Steve felt ashamed,
and angry that he had blushed.

A bunny rabbit raced the truck to the crossroads, and
Steve was in the environs of Carthage, the outskirts of
The Lady of the Lake: Chicago. (Did a stag say, "Woe is
me?") An awkward boy with hair still wet from the faucet over the sink swung onto the truck and shoved himself
halfway through the window, "*Get*-your-*Mor*-ning-*Pa*-per-
here," he caroled, scanning the line as neatly as if he had
taken a course in versification. He did not look at Steve
or the nickel Steve gave him but eyed the prospective cus-
tomers *ad infinitum;* and for each he sang out, "*Get*-your-
Mor-ning-*Pa*-per-here," and sometimes he added, "Read all
about it," *sotto voce.* Steve glanced at the neatly folded
paper. In big letters, jet black and two inches high, he
read, "Rapist Flees."

CHAPTER TWELVE

And in the meantime: I have left Gussie because, and as thoroughly as, Steve has. Steve will never see her again except that one time fifteen years later when he glimpses her waiting for a bus. Steve may have said then, with Jesus, "Woman, what have I to do with thee?" meaning not so much, as Jesus meant, "Our connection was necessary and brief, I am the bridegroom, now, of the church," but something, perhaps, less abstract but just as true, "Something more powerful and passionate made me forget to kiss you good-by; and besides you cheated me out of the fear of aggression. I missed that necessary ritual; I was never a bridegroom, never afraid." And it is true that Steve and Gussie were like a flower with both stamen and pistils; neither caused the other pain, there had been neither aggression or passivity. It had not been a seduction either. No one was possessor, no one possessed. It was more as if he lay in his bed alone; there was just a change of scenery, more variety in his caresses, but the objects he fondled remained subjective; chaste. At least until Mrs. Hooker caught him at it! Perhaps the feeling, only of subjectiveness, is why, when I mention Gussie. to Steve, he insists there was nothing between them, "I loved her, I wanted to marry her, but there was nothing."

"But you said there was; for three years! You said . . . intercourse . . ."

"No! If I said so it was because you expected me to; it's hard to explain."

Yes, it rather is, and I have done the best I can, and might only add that neither had sought the treasure they seem to have found, and to this day do not suspect that it is priceless, and it probably isn't; maybe it is "fool's gold." Each, I imagine, is looking for something else then: some nameless thing, some illusive irregular joy, some unsolved passion; but few of us will be suckled by boulders; and it is improbable that any of these present will find in any grail, holy or despicable, that perfect *anamorphosis*, misbegotten, and unsymmetrical, so perfect in its severe and classic, ideal distortion, planned that way by some Big Idea, that he (or I), smitten in the guts, will feel himself yanked to his knees and praise the Lord. I am trying in a hard way to describe perfection. Can you do any better? Steve and Gussie's well-timed consummation only looked perfect, and civilized man's conception of Beauty only *looks* pretty, and savages know better when they pretend (because they can only pretend) to have found the Thing I have described, in the shape of an irregularly formed stone or bandy-legged root, deliciously grotesque, snub-nosed, sinuous, curtailed. That's when they crown it, set it up with lights and shouts and offer it libations and their own fornication. Because the love of ugliness is very excit-ing, and it only masquerades as such; is that it? waiting for its true love, the one who will know it. And isn't there a terrible deceit in what is called satisfaction?

Well, maybe Steve felt that deceit, and, coupled with violence, topped by Mrs. Hooker like vanilla-flavored cos-mic glue on a dish of tripe, it compelled him toward Car-thage, and purification; via routes 18 and 6; specifically the higher mathematics of abandon and excesses, which is the solution of saints, the dissolution of the average man. There may be other roads to destiny because Fate is as round as an orange, but perhaps a special destiny, if des-tiny is divisible, is part of the powerful desire of our special ones who can take it.

But in the meantime, as I have said, just a word on Mrs. Hooker, from whom Steve has fled as from rape and dis-order of such a powerful kind that it has rendered, I believe the word is, the poor lad as impotent as a ninny, and as defenseless, without his guardian angel, as the rest of us are anyway.

Before the reader's imagination pictures Mrs. Hooker as a fantastic mailed witch in iron jeans with big genitalia and ice cold breasts, plucking the snow-white livers from beardless boys, and frying them over a piercing flame (set off by her cannibalistic passion), consuming their own remains, and using their rose-colored ashes, soft as talcum, on her asparagus bed, let me, in fairness, describe her. She looks, or did look, like any respectable club woman sitting opposite you on the trolley. There is no record of any felony written on her brow or any evil coyness apparent in her bifocaled gaze. She looks as mild as any good cargo ship in harbor, with a comparable displacement, and if you surprised her in the kitchenette she would be scrambling a single-yolked egg and looking merely a little baroque.

But a coincidence, is all I can call it, happened to Mrs. Hooker; caught her up in just the right latitude and longitude, as it were, and, over invisible wires from Chicago, with a good tail wind, came a shattering dream. Her moans awoke the lover of insects and he wanted to give her Jamaica Ginger, but she had had a hotter dose than that and she ordered the deceived husband back to his cot in what had been a closet. He uncomplainingly retired murmuring, *rara avis*, and lying awake for ten minutes, perhaps; because, believe it or not, on his wife's face or somewhere under the covers he had sensed, or seen, a momentary, almost stylish, glamour. Had he, too, been dreaming? of dragonflies? Mrs. Hooker was as good as virgin, you remember; the Professor's interest lay elsewhere on the banks of Eustis Pond. To lie with her would be, in his mind, miscegenation of the crookedest sort.

Mrs. Hooker wept.

Not so much as a woman who has at last given up a life-

time of good works, but as a woman. Denton, uneasy in a
house that housed a thing that was of nature and yet not
of nature, thinking only the obvious, that this was at long
last a menopause, good Lord, on the hearth, gradually
solved it for himself with his watch: he just got up earlier
and came home later.

"Denton," called out Mrs. Hooker appealingly, but he
tiptoed out with his butterfly net and binoculars, mutter-
ing, "Fish, flesh, nor foul nor good red herring," and,
"There's a bee in her bonnet for sure." He skipped aside
to avoid stepping on a group of beetles, tumblebugs, who
were rolling up little balls of dung and pushing them
thither and yon, looking so industrious and serious in their
game, like a lot of little Britishers in homespun, that he
smiled and forgot his wife's predicament. He carried the
image further and laughed out loud because he knew that
the beetles laid their eggs in those little balls of dung.
What looked like fun *was* dead serious! They couldn't
help it! But did the Limeys know!

At first Mrs. Hooker, certainly a woman of character,
that couldn't be canceled in one encounter, tried to put it
out of her mind, but it was one of those dreams that meant
business. It was as if the enemy knew that even the strong-
est battalion nods, that awake they may be invincible,
asleep fallible. It was as if a tutor had decided to educate
a pigheaded pupil during his unconscious and less willful
moments with a gramophone.

There was no doubt that it was Steve, this was not one of

those faceless dreams that leave one comparatively pure; it was as certain as if she had found his identification bracelet under her pillow. She had struggled, hadn't she? but she couldn't look at herself eye-to-eye in the mirror, the great, great granddaughter of professional men in good standing, and lie to herself, even to save the sanity that she had so taken for granted. She studied herself closely, herself and her reflection and said at last humbly, and, I think, profoundly, "There are two Fanny Hookers."

But poor Mrs. Hooker with her paucity of past pleasures gave herself leave to recall after a few hours, then, that other Frances, the depraved one, in the arms of a beautiful and magnetic boy (that lodestar). She felt his soft dark hair on her cheek, his eager sucking lips on the side of her neck; a delicacy and fastidiousness combined with an alluring warmth and confidence thrilled her to pieces; she fell apart. He seemed to lift her with him from the narrow bed almost to the ceiling and curling up in her lap give her generously and happily that dream-protracted intensity of feeling that made up in a matter of moments for all she had missed.

"So that's it."

You may wonder why I put the words of a very young girl in this hardy matron's mouth. But it was the first time it had ever happened to her! Why? Because it had never dared, that's all.

She had never found out that it worked; even her curiosity had been diverted to the whys and wherefores of

hemstitching, detoured to "What makes biscuits rise?"
And now, late, past the meridian, at "that age when
yellow leaves or none or few" she was literally in the
hands of a youngster, of whom she had prophetically but
without understanding said, "He degrades me!" ("Steve?
You?" "That boy is a thief!") She had, without insight
into the passions, been angry at merely a symptom, "He
won't stand up for me." Ahh, Fanny, he lies down with
you now! And when he stands for you, he is as naked and
penetrating as the mast of a ship. And what had Steve
said? "She'd prune me!" That's to be thought about, and
a little more profound. Anyway, he got there first. The boy
she had thought of as a mule, and if she had had the vocabulary, as a half-caste, a hybrid, a marabou (half sailor
and half bishop), who hadn't been good enough for her
Gussie, tucked himself in, now, with her, and, to return
to her New England vocabulary, ruined her. In plainer
words, she had been sabotaged, ravished, scuttled, raped.

It didn't take the sewing woman long to note a change
in Mrs. Hooker who had seemed unchangeable, a kind of
rock, security almost, unimpregnable (I hate to use the
word), in a village of ups and downs, shirt-sleeves-to-riches
kind of place. Like Denton and only a trifle more sympa-
thetic because she was a woman, she said to herself, "The
menopause," and to Mrs. Hooker,

"Hot flashes, deary? I always use an icebag."

"I used to be nineteen inches around the waist without
my corset," Mrs. Hooker answered; and she imagined her-

self a slim and eager girl enthusiastically clinging to her lover, his two hands easily encircling her pliant waist. "Stephan!" she said before she went to sleep, dignifying his name just a little, but stretching herself out on her bed with abandon, raising her toes and sucking in her under-lip. Poor Mrs. Hooker, she longed to experience the sump-tuous and rapturous dream again, but she dreamed only that her teeth fell out. It could not be self-induced.

The humiliation, the jilting, it seemed to her, in her exaggerated frame of mind, was gradual and so harder to bear; anger came slowly and cruelly into her mind where the tantalizing episode lay like an exquisite wound refus-ing to respond to the medication of common sense and fact.

"What's eating her? Entozoön?" (intestinal parasites) thought her bedeviled husband and he tried kindness.

"Put up your dukes," he said, striking a sparring pose, tapping her lightly on her quivering cheek, dancing in a semicircle on his toes.

"Aw, Fan, cheer up!"

She had made a feeble attempt to respond but she felt the years pile up in her as if she were a big bag of laundry and she collapsed on a chair looking something very like that.

"Tea," Denton said uneasily; but while he was boiling the water he planned the last paragraphs of his paper for the Entomology Society in Black Point come next Tues-day. He had witnessed, because he was quiet, off side, talented like a cat, the actual synthesis of a new queen from an adolescent nymph; he had seen how the workers, without much fol-de-rol, had accomplished it, working overtime, he thought, tickled at the idea, without the right to strike (he slapped his thigh). "The *nuerenoptera* have no union," he said out loud, "but," he said, "it wouldn't take them long to manufacture a John L. Lewis, no sir! Few days that's all; few days."

"Denton!"

"Yes, ma'am."

"Listen, Fanny, the toastmaster asked me to stick to my Latin; your old man was a doctor, what's fornicate in Latin?"

A great crimson blush spread over Mrs. Hooker from head to toe.

"Get me my ice-bag," she said, "it's my hot flashes," and she meant it. She lied bravely and it cured her; the courageous denial liberated her. She canceled her order for the new, size forty-two, up-lift bra and the big shirred nylon girdle, the front-interest blouse, and returned to character. Denton, himself, laced her into her old-fashioned corset. And he was glad when she turned on him, "Can't you do *anything*, you fool!" He felt safe again.

"What's this?" he said. In the palm of his hand lay Steve's tarnished identification bracelet.

"Ugh!" said Mrs. Hooker. "That mule again! Embezzler!"

"Atta girl!"

And that's about all of the little saga within the prose of Fanny Hooker's Memoirs, entitled, "Not in Her Wildest Dreams."

CHAPTER THIRTEEN

During the short saga, all she would ever have off the menu, as it were; an *apéritif,* not to be followed by the fixings, or so much as an entree—during the aberration— of his worst enemy, Steve was, it is true, deeply interested in ruin, and, looking up ruin, you will find, *delenda est Carthago.* Steve accosted The Lady of the Lake; he turned her upside down and rifled her pockets, you might say. He longed, it seemed, to vitiate her. But Mrs. Hooker was not actually in his mind the night his spirit so lovingly despoiled her; that, as I told you, was a coincidental coitus. Technicolor blondes and glistening brunettes had to be taken care of, he thought, for their own sakes. Mrs. Hooker's dimensions and composition, her foreshortenings, slid out of his mind to make room for evil that was easier to tangle with; it was a pleasure. It was like taking slim green shoots of aromatic garlic to purify his bowels. The bitter taste of anger that had rendered him impotent changed into a kind of medieval savage hunger; his appetite was restored.

Well, his introduction to *Carthago,* like a footbath one must take before plunging into the pool, was, of all things, Calumet City. His colleagues, eager to show him the town, felt that it was the quickest way to initiate him, and besides, they wanted the pleasure of watching his face. It would be as much fun as taking a virgin, a bobby soxer; a schoolteacher to a tavern. The lawless and ridiculous one-dimensional never-never land called Calumet City is fair comment, I imagine; a place where more is to be seen than felt, and there's nothing there that doesn't meet the eye. It consists of a single street brilliant on either side with pink and orange and blue neon-lighted signs, advertising, of course, girls. The one-way street, because you never retrace your steps, has no corners, no recesses, no alleys, no perspective, no mystery; it is like a plank. One wonders, even, how one gets there, as there seem to be no roads leading into it, and if you ask the way, the person you have asked will most likely say, "It's over there to one side," and will surely say, "It's *parallel* with . . ." That's it, it's analogous rather than real. Your guide will add, "It's sudden like—you can't miss it." I think it isn't *there* in the daytime; it's a midnight phenomenon like a heady dream, and when the cold blinding lights go out, it does, too. It's a mighty funny suburb, without commuters, without dogs, or lawn mowers. I doubt if anyone's address is: Calumet City.

Steve and his new friends did not dress for the occasion and they would have been conspicuous if they had. There are no box seats in this theatre, no privileged minority; neither is one place more amusing than another, or more expensive. Even competition is lacking. Each place is simply an encore of the other one, so close together that you pivot out of one door into the next. The usual distinction between place, joint, and dive doesn't exist either. The drinks, the girls, the music are all excellent. The only variation, perhaps, is in the music offered: hillbilly, jive, popular, and mildly classical. Steve saw and heard for the first time the originals he had only listened to on the radio and victrola. He was rather astonished. "The music is good," he said.

"Of course," they agreed.

"Let's look in here."

Although it was fall and cool, the screen doors had not been removed and before deciding on a place, you just look through the door and take it in first. No one tries to sell you anything; you can stay outside and watch if you like. The others let Steve take a good look. He saw a big naked Amazon as pink as nougat candy step down from a small square platform and walk with long strides, on four-inch heels, toward the door, turn with a flip of an infinitesimal black lace apron on a G-string and disappear. No one had looked up; it was almost as if she was Steve's own private show.

"Not so hot; let's try next door."

Inside they sat against the wall and watched the show. Another big girl as pink and as smooth as the other was undressing to a queer repetitive tune, the beat exaggerated as if a group of backward children were being taught rhythm in the third grade. The thin curved maestro at the piano, turned sideways, looking as if he were cut out of paper, one foot beating it out, watched the girl at close range, a studied lascivious grin on his damp elongated face, an almost obscene disinterestedness about his whole makeup. The girl's expression was as vacuous as a bowl of milk; her eyes moved along the row of working men and clerks who sat at little tables drinking beer, but did not seem to ask or suggest anything. The men went on talking. The ones at the bar nearby were not even looking; nor did they turn on their stools at all, during the stripping, until the master of ceremonies came on in tails and told dirty jokes; that they liked. But Steve looked; his heart beating slow and hard, and his friends watched him closely. The girl took off her bra and showed her beautiful big conical breasts, the nipples a half inch high and shining as if newly shellacked. She raised her hand and with the palm made a circular motion, caressing one nipple. The childish beat of the music went on and on. The girl undid her skirt. Her navel, in the center of her belly like an upside down ceramic bowl, was rouged and deep like a bite. Around her pelvis, that she held forward like a tennis player, she wore a narrow band of velvet with a four-inch, shiny black fringe. Without any change in her expression

and without moving the top of her body, the points of
her breasts could have been painted on two cups hanging
in a cupboard, she tripled the beat of the silly tune with
her hips, buttocks, and vase-like thighs. From the knee
down her stance was like that of a wooden figure. The
silk fringe swung out and in and she spread open her
thighs and thrust herself forward, letting it fondle and
sting her. It became almost unbearable to watch, it lasted
so long and became so insistent. Then the music stopped
quick like the icebox going off and she turned and slid
through a dirty curtain as if she were sinking sideways
into a puddle, her pink bottom quivering with fatigue, a
smudge on the back of one of her muscular calves. A
moment later she hurried out of the place, fully dressed
and not a bit chic, elbowing her way, dying for a cup of
coffee. No one recognized her; she looked like a stenog-
rapher, a little overweight, a little lumpy, not very bright.
She wore loafers on her feet; her heels hidden; her instep
flat. The four-inch-heeled glamour slippers were hanging
on a nail, I suppose, back stage, where the electrician sat
munching a sandwich, watching the bits of powder that
hung in the air, sniffing the Quelques-fleurs, tapping his
foot to the childish tune again.

The three friends counted their change and pivoted into
the next place. Steve had given no sign and no questions
were asked. Almost nostalgically now, the same little aria,
with its soft notes, its persistent beat, permeated the tiny
place along with the smell of beer and sawdust; there

wasn't an ashtray, no rest room, no upkeep. A long secondary bar close to the wall again behind which you sat facing the regular bar; two barmaids, damp and dirty cloths in their fists, slept, their heads on their arms, across it. It was getting late and there was fatigue and nausea in the air; a woman was talking loud and steady without any punctuation, and three workmen enthusiastically discussed politics and bass fishing, hitching up their pants and agreeing with each other, "Jesus, you said it." A pretty girl with a deep frown on her brow sat at the regular bar, sideways, drinking whiskey straight; five little glasses were lined up in front of her, alongside of which she had placed her shoes, a pretty pair of pumps. "Don't like it, do you? Well, what you going to do about it?" she said to the bartender. "What's eatin' you, Sammy, look like you going to cry. What you think he going to do about it?" she asked everybody. Two men on either side of her unostentatiously moved away. She looked directly at Steve, "What *you* going to do about it?"

"We not going to do nothin', Sister," answered one of Steve's friends for him. "Don't tangle with her," he whispered to Steve, "see how everybody's leaving her alone. They get mean. Stay away." The girl brought her small fist down on the bar. "Sure, I'm drunk! You want to make somethin' of it?" She stood up unsteadily and came again at Steve; she seemed to have chosen him. "I don't cry," she said, "not me; cry? Whatsa use, *you* know? Tell me you know whatsa sense of bawlin'? He leaves me and I should cry? No! He goes out. I go out. He gets drunk. I get drunk. Every night he's drunk. So I'm drunk, see?"

"Yes," said Steve gently, "I see."

For a split second a pained and frightened look came over the girl's face, but out of her soft and tremulous mouth came a dirty word, a short and silly, functional word. Steve's friends looked sheepish, but Steve remembered when a dirty phrase had been his only and impotent defense against violence when he felt weakness about to possess him, and he divided his pity between the pretty girl and the little boy. The girl repeated the word softly and laid her head on the bar sideways. You could see the dark roots of her hair at the neck and behind the ears; her cheek was round, almost infantile. She looked like a child sucking its thumb. The bartender picked up her money, and scooped the little glasses into the sink. "You better go home now, Baby," he said kindly. "Yes, Mister, what'll it be?" He wiped up the bar around her methodically. "It's gettin' late, go home now," but she was asleep.

"Take a look, Sonny."

Four nude girls walked along the bar to that tune; four black patches like oblong shadows, was all that they wore, and when they turned, four black strings cut them into two neat halves apiece, behind.

A hefty, broad-backed colored woman with anglican features, dressed in a black riding habit, a crossed skirt, white stock and all the rest, impeccably tailored, a yellow chrysanthemum in her buttonhole, told scatologic jokes in the next place. She spanked her booted legs with an ivory-headed riding crop and accented the epics with an occasional bump; she licked at the sides of her lips and her black eyes pierced the smoky air. "Laugh! You sonsa bitches!"

In another, a really hot trumpet king held the attention of the serious drinkers who had not troubled to look up the legs of the naked girls on the bar or answer their pale blue stares.

"Let's go."

"Try here?"

A sparkling length of neon bulbs spelled out simply "Eugenie"; no come-on; no promises. This really was a king-sized girl as if you were viewing her through a telescopic lens. I suppose she was perfectly proportioned but you couldn't see her all at once to tell, you just had to rearrange the parts, the solids, in your mind; it took time. Besides, she wasn't the varnished kind, she had covered her body all over with pancake powder, must have put it on with a big brush. It had a burnt-orange look, umber and sienna, and her edges were blurred. If I had been there I would have longed for a piece of charcoal to outline her, identify her; take her away from the monotonous background. Contented and sulky, not attempting to dance or gesture, she just seemed to hang there like a tongue in aspic. She had a straight from the shoulder feminine allure. She was woman. All she did was wait. Steve drew in his breath and clenched his fists.

“Like her, Sonny?”

“She’s a bitch!”

A man with a little pleated bag of carpenter’s tools hanging down behind swiveled on his bar stool, “Watch your language, Bud!” and he half rose.

“He don’t mean nothin’,” put in one of the truck drivers. “Come on, let’s get goin’.”

At four o’clock in the morning a fabulous blonde paraded a lengthy lonesome plank in a short chinchilla jacket and a trailing length of scarlet chiffon like the tail of a comet. She undid a rhinestone clasp at her belly and drew the fiery length of material between her powdered legs. Reclasping it, she repeated the performance, letting it stretch out behind her and bringing it through again high up between her fleur-de-lis shaped thighs, caressingly, wickedly. She stared sideways and licked her lips with the tip of her tongue in a circular motion. No one cared. She rode the piece of chiffon, that was continuously in motion, like a witch on a broomstick; it seemed alive, to shudder and glisten and plunge, drawing her after it rather than she, it. It was a clever act. A passionate tune mounted jerkily to a screaming crescendo. Letting go the bright red chiffon, she slipped out of the fur jacket simply by exhaling, and turning her smooth nude back to the unresponsive audience she rhythmically embraced it, the muscles in her buttocks rippling, and, at a furious crashing of cymbals, she drew the soft fur from the front to the back between her legs, tightening herself

together as it came through. Then lifting the furry thing
high, shaking it out, catching up the chiffon, nimbly fast-
ening it, she stomped off like a pony with a plume on his
head amidst no applause whatever.

Dawn on the prairie erased the whole kit-'n-boodle and
hens might have scratched there. Tired men and sickened
men and hopeless men and men of no importance went
home from nowhere. And a hundred girls, their heels
stinging from pumice, their vision blurred with belladonna,
slept, rejuvenating their handsome muscles. The place
was wiped off as slickly as one of the bars with a wet
cloth; all you can eat, all you can feel, all you can take,
for a dollar, as it were.

Steve, not used to late hours and liquor, went fast
asleep and they put him to bed, tenderly. Two hours later
they got him up again, washed him, shaved him, gave him
three cups of black coffee and got him a job.

"So long, Sonny, be seein' you."

CHAPTER FOURTEEN

Calumet City, city of neon and nylon, Steve forgot like an exaggerated and incredible dream. It had been too phoney to touch him. His feelings lay deeper than that. The giant female had troubled him *instanter*, roused his anger; he had wanted to cut her down to size, but even she, so close to the real thing, elemental, and peculiarly desirable and hateful, seemed second-hand and obsolete. She wouldn't do.

He bought a postcard of the Field Museum and addressed it to Anna. He wrote on the back, "I haven't been here," and decided to go.

He joined the slanting silhouettes of people of Chicago who walk leaning forward against a steady wind that seems built in. He soon found that there was no lee-side of the street and the wind is always directly in front of you, no matter what corner you turn. He tried to figure it out but couldn't. Close to the outer-drive he smelled the evil bloody stench of the stockyards, but he didn't know that that was it. He had heard of giant packers with solid gold teeth and had heard of cattle with no place to look but down, but he had not been told of the smell of slaughter; that association he was temporarily spared.

Inside the glistening museum he felt ill at ease as if he were looking into a crystal ball at something that was none of his business. He saw a strange and everlasting survival of creatures restored and shellacked, feathered, and painted to resemble themselves. Each seemed to own a plot of his own with glamorless sodden grass and an indigenous tree with ersatz bark, a weighted trunk and leaves that had to be dusted. He saw birds with everything but the song, and shameless elastic worms, the story of their migration printed on a sign for everyone to see.

And man, the animal, was there, too; genuine to the simulated pubic hair and raised light blue veins crossing and recrossing the forearms and insteps. If you opened a little door in his neck you could see his jugular vein as good as new. He was all there in his progression, if you like, from cave-man to panty-waist. Nothing is left out and one imagines his heart, lungs, and bowels are in the right place. But in spite of a thorough-going immodesty and scientific trustworthiness, encyclopedic detail, foot-notes, and addenda, with cross references, the thing was missing. The good stout parts were there, all right, but sex had been, either by oversight, some sort of misunder-standing, or censorship, omitted. A kind of terrible ster-ility, like punishment, was portrayed, and Steve wondered why. At least he felt that something important was missing, that it wouldn't work the way it was, and maybe a mechanism in the basement was the answer. He saw the leaden-jawed Neanderthal and his passionless spouse and couldn't understand it. A real dog got in and sniffed at the hard man's knees and his hair raised up on his shoulders; he ducked his head and looked at Steve questioningly, the tip of his tail moving uneasily.

"Good dog," said Steve, "it's me."

The dog joyously nuzzled and fondled him, the saliva dripping off his long tongue.

"No dogs *allowed*," called a thin voice and an agitated guard in a blue uniform with braid hurried in.

"Look at the sign, sir," he said sternly. "It says, 'no dogs allowed.' " He took out his handkerchief and wiped the Neanderthal man; he peered at three drops of saliva on the shining floor and went for a mop.

"Come on, friend," said Steve and the dog gladly followed him, twisting and turning and licking his fingers as if to say, "My, the smell of you relieves my mind, pal."

"But if sex isn't allowed here, neither is death," thought Steve, if not exactly in those words, if in any words at all. "The whole thing smacks of bravado; it is a graveyard and not a graveyard. 'Ashes to ashes and dust to dust' is not heard intoned in this cemetery and God isn't necessary."

On the way out, in the foyer, on a fluted pedestal, there was a big vase of beautiful two-toned roses; a printed

notice read, "The Eleanor Roosevelt." On a level with
his nose, Steve sniffed at them and they scratched his
cheek, but it wasn't the thorns, it was the starched and
laundered piqué they were so cleverly made from. Over
and above poised a great bald eagle with crazy myopic
glass eyes. A little moth flew out of his breast and did
wing overs in a ray of sunlight. The dog raised his leg
against the fluted pilaster topped by "The Eleanor Roosevelt" and smiled at Steve.

"No! No!" said Steve. "Wait for the park."

The dog agreed and jauntily preceded Steve outside.
"We're going to the park; we're going to the park," he
told everybody. On the stone steps, oblivious of the sun,
the wind, the smell of the stockyards, a girl and a boy
clung together drinking from each other's mouths some
powerful anesthetic that relieved them of the tension of
taboo, the taboos Steve and the dog had just witnessed in
the museum: sex, death, and God. They were students
and the pages of Aristotle and Galileo fluttered in the
wind while they searched for perfection elsewhere.

In the park the two of them daydreamed. The dog,
eons away really, pointed at multicolored and obese
pigeons that settled on the grass; they twitched and hustled
away from his bogey-man stare only to circle him and
return. Steve, in broad daylight, the pupils of his eyes
reduced like the shuttered lens of a good camera, quickly
straddled the hateful image of an umber and sienna
blonde. He brutally spread her out as if she were to be

vivisected and fastened himself upon her like a leech. That pungent and porous glamour woman who had hung in the grimy air over the bar at Calumet City was domiciled now in the frontal lobes of Steve's brain like a pendulum in a clock. He deflowered her in his imagination one sunny afternoon in the park and slapped her when he was through. "Skit! Slut! Doxy!" I suppose he said. The dog looked in his face and questioned him; faintly moving his tail.

"Ahh," said Steve.

All Hell broke loose! A black sedan raced down Michigan Avenue followed by another identical black sedan. People started running; women screamed; little boys hung on to their private parts. The gunfire was like popcorn in a canyon. Steve saw tongues of flame spit out from the twin sedans and then he heard, seconds later, pop! pop! pop! pop! The pigeons rose up like a huge umbrella and hung in the air waiting for it to be over. Almost immediately it was. The scene settled down again like a pool when the stone has sunk to the bottom. But a cop stood in front of Steve; he stared uneasily in the direction the black sedans had taken and ran a thumb along his chin; you could hear it, like static. In a business-like way he turned to Steve, "Got a license for your dog?" he said.

"What was the shooting?" asked Steve.

"I said got a license for your dog?" the cop repeated firmly.

"I haven't got a dog," Steve said.

"Oh, *wise* guy," said the policeman; he reached for his little book and licked a stub of pencil, but then he seemed to change his mind.

"Stranger in town?"

"Yes, sir."

"Keep movin'," said the cop.

The dog had waited out the decision with good grace, looking away into the distance, his tongue hanging out; and he did not hold it against Steve that he had momentarily denied him. He led Steve along the outer drive and for a while raced and played and stalked and dug holes with another nameless mongrel while Steve looked at the crude drawings and paintings in house paint on the big slabs of stone along the shore. Some were merely initialed; others bore the names of girls and boys: Jeannette and Tom; Phyllis and Jim; then there were clubs: The Blue Devils; The High Flyers; The Foxes. There were assignations: F.S. meet J.L. at Winkie's; and bold landscapes, not bad; some fishes; a big cat. On a tall flat slab freshly painted, still uncensored by time or eroded by the spray, was something special, conceived by a sly joker, part artist, part lecher. It was a student-girl divided straight down the middle by a sure hand. The left side of her was dressed in a cap and gown and in her hand she held a diploma; the tassel on her cap was correctly placed; the right half of her was naked and painted in a luscious pink. The slight roughness of the stone gave the work of art a real flesh quality and the contrast with the black gown was startling and provoking. The bare breast and thigh, the half belly, seemed especially immodest and inviting, almost insolent, although the face was placid and unsmiling, a little arrogant. I wonder if Steve felt a kinship with the artist: just see what is in the power of man to do to woman! I've no doubt the original of that girl with higher grades will pass herself tomorrow on the way to classes and blush, blush to see herself everlastingly half naked with one pink breast, one tremulous thigh, one half navel; bisected as surely and neatly as if she had been raped. Steve made plans in his mind as he looked. This evil invitational drawing was like a route number pointing the way, advising him. His dream-girl, that he had left home to violate, was becoming a tormenting *idée fixe* and there was no doubt in his mind that he would accomplish his mission again and again. It can hardly be expected that he thought of it as a purifying measure; he was not given the perspective of his life as I, as his biographer, have been. He did not hear that voice from the clouds that St. Augustine heard, "Nevertheless such shall have trouble in the flesh, but I spare you." But Steve, as surely as he, had had a summons from that other selfless self, his soul, "Do this for me," and he would because he was compelled to. No sweet white cumulus to guide him, but an almost continuous pinkish smog containing the condensed, diluted, and vaporish blood of countless cattle and the exhalations of confounded sons of pioneers, the rice pow-

My Hero

———

189

der from the cheeks and armpits of their women and frails; and gunpowder too; instrument weather, making Chicago hard to find unless you really wanted to. Well, he did. He had left undone the pouting Amazon at Calumet City because he felt, you remember, she wouldn't do.

Part of this procrastination, evasion maybe, is Steve's; part mine, because I love him and don't relish, because I am not a saint, "the beguiling service of devils," or care to dwell, as they have, on that "torrent of pitch . . . the monstrous tide of foul lustfulness"; and part in his stars.

And as if he knew it he went next to the Planetarium where they sell stars and mortgage the moon, putting aside for a little while that half-woman on the shore, but cut in half as she was, one side of him pink and tender and voluptuous as she, the other in the shadow of—call it indecision; abortive metamorphosis, it looked like. So he sat for a quarter of a dollar under synthetic stars, under a milky opaque man-made phenomenon, a galaxy of cold light as cold as neon at Calumet City. He watched a gibbous moon decline and set and rise again, and Venus, the color of a Florida orange, rotate in a weatherless ersatz sky, as nude as a tinted tennis ball. At least the round dome and pure disinfected light smelled of nothing-ness and the temperature had been figured out beforehand. A neat-as-a-pin professor turned the stars and the sun and the phases of the moon on and off and showed him the star of Bethlehem and the revolving frustrated parallel sun at the pole, and rainbows, too, and comets. On a winter's evening he was treated to an impressive summer sky. He saw Boötes and Arcturus and Corona Borealis (will any good come of it!) ; he saw his own constellation, Virgo, with the big blue-white first magnitude star indenting her pelvis, apparently. Will an influence one hundred and twenty light years away penetrate the lecherous smog I have described? Can any patient man in any tower of whatever frequency talk the Virgin in? The professor's enthusiasm began to wane like one of his obedient puppet moons but he was conscientious and crowded into the last ten minutes: a shower of meteors, the nine moons of Saturn, the origin of the solar system, the Pleiades on the shoulder of the Bull, some asteroids, Halley's Comet on the morning of May 13, 1910, and again in 240 B.C., and just for fun because his present audience wouldn't be there, in 1986 (he gave the impression that he would be, however). It all ended finally with a charming lunar halo that made the ladies gasp. The professor wiped his brow and bowed. He reached out and turned on the make-believe daylight, so powerful and even that every last little shadow retreated into the corners and was absorbed into the walls. "Thank you for your attention," he said. "I think I have demonstrated the wonders of pure science and the absurdity of any belief no matter of how long-standing in that pseudo, so-called science of astrology. There is absolutely no evidence. Thank you. Good night. Remember if there is inclement weather tomorrow, there is always fair weather in the Planetarium. Ha, Ha!"

"Be seein' you," he said to the electrician, and he was off to less stellar regions with his memoirs, his manuscript, and the slab of chocolate he kept in his pocket to build up the energy he had spent on the stars.

Well, Steve had got his money's worth; indeed he might as well be dead; he had seen everything backwards and forwards. He had seen with the naked eye the passage of time and the seasonal patterns as easy as a rotating pie; there was nothing left for him to imagine; he was not Archimedes who said if there was some place to stand he could lift the earth, knowing what he did about specific gravity and leverage from the simple observations he had made in his own bath.

Outside he heard some one say stuffily, "It's very unusual in these parts." The real honest-to-goodness northern lights streaked the sky like peppermint candy, like neuralgia in the heavens. "They take place in a vacuum," the voice said, "they are essentially electric."

"It looks like inside the Planetarium," a woman said, but most of the crowd didn't even look up. Steve felt uneasy and irritated; he had had enough of the pure unadulterated inner sights of Chicago, scientific as Hell, but it wasn't likely that his aspic dream-girl would come to him of her own accord, but she did.

"People are funny," she said. He felt her warm quivering thigh against the side of his leg, she stood so close, "when it's free they don't look."

A cop came up the steps and looked at them standing alone. "Keep movin'," he said.

"Pretend you know me, Stupid," she whispered, "call me Adèle."

"Look Sister," said the cop, "I've seen you before. I told you."

"I'm goin'," said the girl sulkily.

Steve stood still but kept her in view under the street lights. She walked—I can only describe it as two steps back to one forward. Her whole body seemed to wait. The dog came bounding up the steps with a sort of "where *have* you been" in his look but Steve said, "Go home!" sharply, and the dog turned and went to whatever meeting place dogs go to when you say, "Go home," and really mean it. And Steve meant it; where he was going was no place for a nice dog. The dog had shown him the sights just as his colleagues en route had introduced him to a kind of synthetic depravity just for fun, made news, almost, in Calumet City; and in his own mind, too, he had had his more serious previews. But this was it.

"It isn't free," the girl said cheerfully, referring back to the display in the heavens that had been slighted on the steps of the Planetarium.

She was no flirt and opened her legs. "Hurry up," she said.

Steve knew how because he had planned it that way, and so it wasn't a transport of love or a timid manifestation either. It was lust at its best. He bit his lips lest he kiss her and like an incensed and deadly snake he struck like distilled lightning at a detested enemy, and let go of his venom, nearly swooning in the sweetness, the terrible sweetness, of his revenge; it was a vicious vendetta in his mind; life's blood for life's blood; insult for insult. How he had saved up this voluptuous incestuous insult and how he loathed the pretty little vessel that had volunteered her services! He shuddered with pleasure in the act. But he recoiled at once when the thing was finished, like that serpent that has bitten and discharged its poison and is empty. He just had time in the greed of his performance to whisper fiercely in her ear, "Bitch!"

"You're a brute!"

Even this girl who had not expected tenderness felt a sickening humiliation, sensed the depth and power and viciousness of the physical and moral insult. But Steve felt no compassion for a disheveled little prostitute, stained and bruised by him and tearful and childishly angry at her inability to retaliate; a pitiable enough sight to the unprejudiced.

"Now I can go back," he thought. "It's gone."

He emptied his pockets too and threw his evil savings on the bed.

"Thanks," he said.

"Get out."

But he didn't go home because it wasn't gone. He wasn t through. He had miscalculated. He wasn't healed. It would take time.

Outside, as he walked away the rest of the night, the faint reflection of the northern lights could still be seen, almost heard, like the crushing of a paper napkin, because Chicago had finally gone to bed and slept. A pure cold wind came up out of the north over Lake Michigan and the tall city with thousands of lighted windows in the empty towers was a pretty, almost delicately lovely sight. That behind each window a scrubwoman, like Lady Macbeth, desperately attempted to clean up is only an afterthought. Steve accepted the beauty of the mirage-like city by the lake and it added to his feeling of well-being; he thought he was cured, that he had performed the ritualistic act, that the thing had been attended to; that psychic euphoria that comes to the aid of the very sick came to him. He went to bed and slept; a good boy.

"It was foul and I loved it," St. Augustine had said but being a Saint he sustained the idea further, "And I became to myself a carrion land." "I stole the beautiful and luscious pears with my lewd companions for the joy of stealing and threw them to the very hogs" was the thrilling confession of a symbolic and vicious rape the Saint couldn't enjoy, and what he pilfered he made a present of to the poor unfortunate beasties whom Jesus, knowing their social status, dignified somewhat with devils and self-destruction, attributes heretofore of man alone. Poor truly swine, representatives of filth as far back as they pleased to domicile themselves in a creamy consistency of earth and excrement, a homestead mixture peculiar to them alone, abhorred even by other beasts. But the hogs and sows dream of truffles, and their obscenity is involuntary.

Steve woke and reported for work as usual the next morning, with no left-overs in his mind, either of a bad dream or plaguing actual experience. The dog knew, without being given the address, where he worked, and joined him in the cab of the truck, leaning far out to enjoy everything at once and loving the feel of his breath forced back down his throat in the strong relative breeze they made for themselves. He seemed to swallow his tongue again and again and his eyeballs flattened out and the hair parted on his chest and rippled and tickled. All this and a master, too; like a woman with husband and lovers as well. Steve told his boss he was quitting in three days and promised the dog he would spend the last day with him.

That last day, that turned out to be not the last day, they spent in their favorite places and did some sightseeing as well. They looked at Nathan Hale, in bronze, as cats, and dogs, too, may look at kings and images of kings. That king-sized Hale, so expensive, who has been innocently defiled by unthinking pigeons, and with the sweet young look on his face, "I am sorry I have but one life to give for my country." One imagines him saying it without any schizophrenia or heroics whatever; genuinely sorry that he may not love but once.

Steve went through the Aquarium while the dog waited outside, and sent Anna a blue postcard of an electric eel. The fish eyed him sideways as he strode through the place, his hair curling in the sweet-smelling humidity of the breath, almost, of live fish; his mind as placid and platonic as theirs, but his heart's blood warm and dangerous. He smiled at the simple-minded octopus whose disinterested embrace could have put an end to his career and his progeny, and gave a cursory glance at the silly little cuttle-fish who manufactured without any malice at all a substance more dangerous than the sword.

It doesn't seem fair that you, the reader, and I, the biographer, are aware of what is going to happen to this good Steve by nightfall; that he can make no preparation, or fight against, if he cared to, the inevitable return of passion that has by no means been liquidated or spent; that scarcely out of the domain of animals that act like drawings and who thrive and produce without copulation or satisfaction he will again be solicited and eagerly accept an opportunity to despoil a chimera that has a trick of returning every three days and lying down to be tormented by a knight who wears even less armor than she, but who carries a powerful shining sword for her alone. And the pretty Phoenix is vain of an exquisite wound that will never heal and bleeds in time with the moon, an insignia of magic and mystery; an alluring mastery over bigger and wiser logicians and stubborn thinkers, as well as those timorous savages I told you about.

There were women who were as sensually strong as he and who delighted in his savagery and the weapon he concealed on his person, and there were those who did not thank him for his arrogant male charm. He felt that he wasted his hate on the former, the latter's humiliation and abasement, her shame, not only at not being loved which she scarcely expected, but being despised, suiting the mood he deliberately fed in his mind on a bitter cerebral aphrodisiac. He was cutting the big sulky lion-colored aspic woman down to size because she swung there like a pendulous booby-trap (Mrs. Hooker in a disarming disguise indeed!). How could he know, even if he could recall the target of his original compulsion, that Fanny had swallowed her hot dosage bravely, had done her time, had had her share of insult, had been raped in a dream and jilted, too, all in the relative ratio of time between actual happenings and dreams. Perhaps it was Steve, then, who was dreaming; it was taking him so long with the chimera, while Mrs. Hooker, as it were, had had the shortest and pleasantest night of the year.

From the *cordon sanitaire*, the weatherless but humid fish-house, Steve, in search, he thought, of shiny postcards for the pure one at home, Anna, proceeded, dog at heel, to the Art Institute where the cement lions outside curved their weighty tails in a very good casting job and girls in smocks and boys in jeans also decorated the entrance to acceptable beauty, insured and guarded and dusted daily and recommended by a distinguished trusteeship. It wasn't so much, in fact very little at all, the nudes he looked at in gilded frames, or the sensuous vigorous coloration of the impressionists and the brainy perverse distortions of line by sophisticated painters, it was just the passage of time; the hands of the clock on the wall. It was only a coincidence again that he stood in the reflected light of one of Renoir's pink trees that looked so much like flesh and veiled blood vessels, and "woman" stood there again in his willing brain. For a sickening second he remembered his self-censored childhood and the brown boy-locusts clinging to the flesh-like trees, too, in that queerly sacred wood with its golden bough of mythology and extravagance, and he wanted for one second, only that: that irresponsible exciting stimulation without any aftermath; the purity of afterwards. Arbor Day.

"Pretty?" she said.

His heart pounded because it was time for it to pound but the girl procrastinated.

"Do you want the usual thing?" she said. "Or something special?"

"The usual thing," said Steve. "Now."

The girl stood off and looked at him, a little sneer curving her red lips, "Oh, from the sticks," she said. "Not me then," and she started away. "Fancy meeting you here," she trilled and he felt as if she had spit on him. He saw her round buttocks moving away from him and he wanted to split her in two like an apple, viciously, and hurl the bloody halves as far as he could, perhaps to the very hogs!

The square softly lit room was empty of anyone but the antagonists. Steve grasped her thin arm and pulled her around.

"Look out! Stop it!" she said.

"You little bitch," he said out loud and he shoved her right shoulder away with a quick slap, at the same time pulling her forward briskly with his other arm so that her pelvis came forward and she had to cling to him with her legs to keep her balance; he felt that her knees were bare, and her hips, too, felt slippery under her skirt. The girl threw her head back.

"So corny!" she said, but her eyes shone. "O.K., keep your shirt on!"

"Go home!" said Steve harshly as he came out with the girl.

"What!" she said. "Whose dog is that?"

"I don't know," said Steve, and the dog sat down and looked off toward Lake Michigan so as not to embarrass his master. He watched him and his strange new friend until he lost sight of them in the five o'clock home-going crowd, and loped off to that limbo. Well. . . .

CHAPTER FIFTEEN

And so Steve thought with his blood. To Carthage he had unerringly come, hadn't he; and all around in his ears a cauldron of unholy loves (to paraphrase St. Augustine once more). You can find these words if you like in the Chicago Public Library, "And I boiled over in my fornications." But the Saint added, "And Thou heldest thy peace." Well, no one interfered with Steve's pleasures either.

I don't want to tell you all he did but he did it all; he searched for the evil witness in all kinds of places and in duplicate Delilahs and Jezebels and he did the thing he knew how to do, good. He meant to get over his shame, vindicate himself forever, and he was well on his way; the worst was over.

He wasn't bored by repetition of the act and he might have gone on and on except that it wasn't going to be like that. His passionate behavior at least was straight and sure and so assuaged and chastened itself. He knew little of, and did not practice, perversion: the roundabout-way, the fancy alleviation of procrastination and tricks. The girls and the men, too, who had offered him their funny lullabies, their weird intercourse, in a wonderland of waiting and interchange, almost, of state, peculiar diversified masqueraded loving, applied fornication with wide open eyes, he refused. The thin girl in the Institute of Beauty who had meant to tease him by her invitation to "something special" had not picked her man carefully and was wasting her artistic talent. Steve treated her to his own technique without parentheses or ceasural pauses, or distortion of line, a perfectly natural process that bored her to death. Neither was he interested in or in any way tempted by those quarter-smiles on the lips of ironic men that other men admire, that captain's walk, that pelvic arrogance, that strangely enough woman's grace behind. These oblique grown-ups did not remind him of the poetic friendship of his adolescence; it wasn't the same; it was too terrible, too sad, it had nothing to do with him. Besides, his compulsion left him no time for sexual sight-seeing. The preserved Africans, the cold-pack Neanderthal man and spouse of the museum of hygiantics, and the frigid fauna of the aquarium rested him, on the other hand, and the dog's generous devotion kept him a little in touch with goodness, like a little black and tan mongrel Cerberus tending his favorite soul until bigger help came. And Steve began to show the dog some affection, too.

"Good dog!" "Come here, boy."

The consuming danger of pleasure unattended by sen-

timent was passing maybe, but not integrated. He hated
woman still for all his physical pleasure in her, and he
stroked the dog's head softly and gently.

"Good night, pal."

Poor Steve, he made the most, too, of that aggression
Gussie had unwittingly denied him in their bisexual, almost, love; that intermixture of stamen and pistils, as if
a breeze had accomplished the orgasm, when she did not
know she had been seduced nor he either. He defied again
and again that young man's coming-of-age fear that she
had not given him a chance, somehow, to feel, so that his
first woman had never really been his. But now these first
women seemed interminable and he no longer anticipated
a fear or felt it. His wedding night was successfully over,
with numberless unloved but satisfactory brides. And he
felt no choice, either, between technicolor blondes or glistening brunettes; his pupils did not dilate, because he did
not look, at an occasional redhead with pink skin and
cerulean eyes. ("Hurry up!" "What seems to be the
trouble?" "Well, what are you waiting for?") There was
no dalliance, no soft impeachment, only pleasure with a
double meaning for Steve.

But a kind of nausea built up in him, coexistent with
desire, at the sight of a naked woman no matter what
color she was. He closed his eyes, and struck, and an even
more terrible sweetness poured out of him like hot honey,
until less and less he thought of evil and hate, and he
quit. It was really over.

“I’m going to take you with me, feller; tomorrow,” said
Steve.

“Oh boy!” thought the dog. “Well, we’ll see.”

“Got a light?”

The last bitch (in Steve’s life) stepped out, it seemed,
of nowhere, as the trumped up temptations do of fasting
saints in caves and deserts, with no visible transportation
or sustenance; as if they were born of their own starving
bellies and aching loins.

“No, thanks,” said Steve.

“It’s not for money,” said the girl.

“I have no money,” said Steve impatiently.

“You aren’t listening,” she said, and added imperiously,
“Send your dog home, I don’t like dogs.”

“I’m not interested,” said Steve.

“Listen,” she said. “I don’t want anything. I’m just
lonely and you look nice.”

Steve felt an irritation in his chest as if there was too
much starch in his shirt.

This little dialogue with pictures took place just after
Steve and the dog had left the Fifty-ninth Street Station
and were walking through the park, just to see what the
University looked like, and pass the time until morning
when Steve really and truly, this time, was going home,
and the dog really and truly had come to believe him.

“Sit down here and let’s talk,” the girl persisted.

“No.”

"Honey, don't let's fight it; I know a place real near by."

Steve's hatred was gone and this time it was dangerous. The girl's sweet voice sent a long thin pain down into his loins and an involuntary desire lifted him up.

"Christ," he pleaded.

The girl, her eyes upon him, had not missed anything, and knew she must act quickly. It was true she was not looking for money; she had restlessly come out for just this, and her heart leapt, her eyes shone; she was pretty, too. She lovingly, almost respectfully, placed one hand on the center of Steve's yearning and with the other lifted her skirt until the soft orange light of the park lamp warmed her upper thighs and sent deep shadows into deep places; her bright red mouth opened and curved up as if she were in a kind of smiling and exquisite pain. Steve felt a terrible longing in his guts that almost drew him to his knees, but he was spared; his head remained clear, his body obeyed him and he jumped out of her embrace as if she had given birth to him. But he did not strike her, he did not spit on her, he did not call her a dirty name.

"You'd better go home" is all he said. "It's late." The dog lifted his head.

"No, not you, pal."

"You're cruel," the girl said, almost sobbing at the little bit of kindness in his tone, and I suppose he was. Anyway, that was all there was to that incident in the succulent park; that park dimly lit for lovers and libertines, a chance to make good or disintegrate; a kind of wind tunnel just to see, maybe, if your wings will really stick.

Steve didn't know he had changed; he wasn't proud exactly; it was something extraneous. Could it be Virgo? Libra? The dog?

They went down that midway that had once been a bawdy circus and looked at something they couldn't have: Education. But they did not know enough to miss it or envy the boys and girls and professors who supposedly and maybe did keep their minds on other things. The halls of learning, I think they're called, were dark except for an occasional isolated light; a big cathedral, Steve thought it was, mounted ponderously into a certain amount of sky, and throaty but meticulous organ music came out of it like, and unlike, harmony, as if it were breathing. Round and round a cluster of handsome Gothic buildings, tenderly caressed by new ivy, and not yet colored by time or harassed by too much weather, a shiny police car circled, the shortwave phrases and hot jazz intermingling, seeing to it, one supposes, that nothing horrid got inside. Steve did not know he was passing a girl's dormitory and he looked up when he felt a shadow across a lighted window. He saw the figure of a girl, but only half of her. She was divided in two from head to toe. She was standing still, looking in a mirror, perhaps. It was the dressed half of the painted schizophrenic on the outer drive! Half a cap and half a gown, half a face with half a mouth. But he could not see if the look resembled the sulky arrogant one of the half-student, half-harlot, on a slab of stone by the lake. Surely, though, it was the very girl! and he imagined the other half of her as if he had painted her himself: the round pink breast, the half belly, the split thighs, the one curving leg and knee, a bare foot with red polish on the toes! He even improved on the original. He only stared for a moment but he knew well her thesis and her signature; as well, too, as if he, himself, had written it.

"Whore," he said.

But he said it without enthusiasm; an almost disinterested last impulse, not any longer a true compulsion, scarcely shook him. And perhaps that particular word, that unembittered name-calling was significant of something in the pattern of his own story as I see it. "Whore" means to fornicate; to practice idolatry, not so much a Freudian error in some dictionary but a mythological inheritance, because in those dear dead days maidens prostituted themselves in praise of Dionysus, "squatting outside the gates of the city in fornication" (for the love of God!); I didn't make it up.

Some line of thought, some equalization of pressures, led Steve to just the right church on the south side of Carthage and he stepped in. It was almost dark inside, the high windows letting in a minimum of striped violet light, a left-over glow from the city. Near the altar he saw a life-size image of Mary, sweet in the face, with rosy lips, fine brows, and dimpled chin, holding a calcimined doll Jesus with a pink tipped penis and blue eyes. She was dressed in nylon and scallops, and cheap lace, and there were artificial flowers in her hair and pinned to her home-made dress. The jumpy light of fat candles at her feet sent hovering shadows across her cheeks and gave her a startling realness. Steve did not like the thing and turned away; but as he walked back down the side aisle he was fortunate enough to make out in the semi-darkness, along the walls, Faggi's meditative stations of the cross, so deeply religious, so moving, the line so pure. He studied them all and wanted more; he returned, passed the girl Mary, *jeunesse doré*, in her pathetic finery and found to one side in the queer twilight an unlighted Mary, a dark Mary, a deep, aloof Mary, with her dead man stretched over her parted knees. (The Pietà, also by Faggi.) The very drapery mourned; the elongated face and high forehead, the narrow lips, the beautiful long nose and parted hair, the delicately poised hands with rounded finger tips caught Steve in his insides and this time he was pulled to his knees.

"Lovely woman," he whispered.

He sat in the church a long time wondering, but no logic came to him. A sweet smell, sensuous, intense, hung in the air and seemed to be glutting the candles, taking away the oxygen; it was yesterday's incense that smells of love and of death and penetrates the human heart. Steve repeated again, "Lovely woman," and it meant more to him and to us than "Ave Maria" or "Mystical Rose"; but he leaned his head a moment against the pew and he might have said, "*Mea maxima culpa*," but I don't think so. Steve was really no saint, but an errant angel, perhaps, and felt no thrill, simply wonder. Still, he should have been accompanied by litanies and cherubs as he left the church, because Mary had done it again, Faggi's Mary, not the little impostor, and he felt rested and good. He was humming as he came out to join the dog, a tune that didn't fit the occasion, or maybe it did, I don't know. "And around the dear ruins each wish of my heart . . . ," that's all he knew.

The dog sniffed at him and growled very low, and at the same time faintly wagged his tail as if he couldn't make up his either end. His brain and his intuition were at odds.

"Why, feller, it's me!" Steve laughed. "I suppose it's the incense," he thought.

A scream like a roman candle seared the night.

A single shot bit into the density that followed it.

Then in the slack silence they heard and saw a man running toward them. He was crouched forward, his arms swinging, like a gorilla, and he was weaving back and forth across the sidewalk like a terrorized animal; a rodent trying to get away from the shadow of the hawk. Hunted!

Three police rounded the corner; two came after him from behind, and closed in.

"Sweet Jesus," the black man said. "I didn't do it!"

Two young men, hatless, came running.

"He attacked the girl!"

"He shot her escort!"

"No! No!" said the black man, falling to his knees, his eyes rolling, his teeth chattering.

"Get up, you!" said one cop.

The man struggled upwards but his knees sagged.

"Before God, I didn't do it!"

"He's reaching for a gun!" said another cop suddenly.

The third cop said, "No you don't!" and shot him in the stomach. The blood ran down his legs.

It was finished and it was obscene. The chapel carillon began to ring and the din and the blood was horrible.

That night Steve's guardian angel came back; she held him in her arms and he loved her. It did not seem queer that her face was featureless. It was chastity again and for good, nameless.

CHAPTER SIXTEEN

The dog liked the new look, the look I called the divine look, on his master's face, and couldn't keep his eyes off him. He sat on the curb oblivious of all the tantalizing smells and sudden motions of the city and watched Steve check the big truck. It did seem that he was almost fondling it, and he did talk to the engine, "Good girl," he said.

"Come on!"

He didn't even say good-by to The Lady of the Lake or thank her for the bread and butter and heady wine she had served him; it had been highly seasoned bread, and sweet butter, but he was thinking of shoofly pie and apple pandowdy.

Their trip home was without incident, except a pretty one. The Sisters were in the field, this time preparing the ground for sowing, and he saw her again, the one who had made him blush. He drew alongside of the road and leaned out of the cab.

"Hi!"

The Sister straightened up and looked at him without surprise.

"Good morning!" she sang out.

All the others, as if it were a ballet, straightened up and looked at him too.

"Good morning," they called.

Steve had a generous desire to give the girl something; he reached up and drew out one of Anna's postcards; it was a shiny view of the Planetarium.

"Thank you!"

"You're so pretty!" Steve said.

"Good-by," and they all waved.

"So long."

"I'm sorry," the Sister said quickly, "I couldn't say 'good morning' to you the last time, but it was time for me to be silent."

As they drove along monotonously Steve suddenly thought out loud, "If she knew what I was thinking she'd prune me!" And he laughed, a cheery and good laugh. There was nothing in his mind of Mrs. Hooker's nasty philippic on dirty boys; and the dog smiled broadly and wiggled himself.

Time and space passed away beneath the able strong tires of the truck and New England began to appear alongside their migration and familiar aspects turned up. Steve thought to himself, "It's been a long time." (That short winter!)

As he came into his own village he slowed down while
a bus ahead of him stopped; "Stop!" it said. He saw
Gussie waiting for it. She was pregnant and wore an old
coat; but her slim pretty legs were shining in nylon
stockings and as the bus driver drew up for her she gave
him a beguiling, happy, irresponsible smile and climbed
nimbly in.

"It's fifteen years, at least," Steve thought. "It's got to
be," and he thought a little while about his youth and of
Gussie. "I didn't harm her," he said and he meant it. He
felt a mild nostalgia and thought gently of old times; of
John; of his first job.

He was home and he went into the living room. Anna
sat facing him at the piano picking out a tune with one
finger. It had a tinkling, repetitive series of simple notes.
It was that tune. But Steve didn't think of the shimmering
naked women that it should have provoked in his mind.

"Anna, you little stinker!" he said lovingly, and she
hung around his neck with her whole weight.

"Stevie!"

Well, last night I decided my story was finished and I
let Steve read it. I was nervous and he is a slow reader.
Now and then he would look at me as I sat tensely staring
at his face, a long look that I could not fathom. At last,
it was after midnight, he finished.

"Why, there's not a word of truth in it!" he said, the
soul of honor shining in his eyes.

"Steve!"

"It isn't me."

"Why, Steve, if I hadn't told you it was you, you would sue me!"

"Well, it's good, anyway."

"Thank you, Steve, dear," I said but I wondered: Perhaps this is all my violence, my fears, my anger, even my language. And Steve, who is so silent; I might say I only know what he hasn't told me.

But an hour later before he left me he said,

"Do you still love me now that you know all about me?"

"Oh, yes, Steve," I said happily.

"What an imagination!" he laughed.

"Of course," I said tentatively, "I can't hope to compete with your guardian angel."

"No," he said quite seriously.